A H

Elizabett MacDonad

A
HOUSE
OF
CARDS

Elizabeth MacDonald

Pillar Press

Copyright © 2006 Elizabeth MacDonald

A House of Cards
First published 2006
Pillar Press
Ladywell
Thomastown
Co. Kilkenny

www.pillarpress.ie

ISBN 0955082137

British Library Cataloguing in Publication Data.
A CIP catalogue record for this book is available
from the British Library.

Printed in Ireland by Betaprint

10 9 8 7 6 5 4 3 2 1

For my Italian family, Luca and David Marcus, and my Irish family, Mairéad, Marcus, Randal, Marcus P.B. and Sarah

ACKNOWLEDGEMENTS

Heartfelt thanks to my husband Luca for his unstinting support and patience; to Stephen Buck at Pillar Press, and my editor Marian O'Neill, for their skill and expert advice; to Sarah MacDonald, sister in a million, for giving so generously of her time and know-how; to Fausto Ciompi for sharing his knowledge of Tuscan history; and to Mario Luzi – *maestro* and inspiration.

Amor non tenet ordinem
– attributed to St. Columbanus

CONTENTS

Introduction xi
Preface xv
No Man Is an Island 1
Wisteria 14
Fireworks 27
Babele 38
Falling Stars 52
A House of Cards 63
Sunday Lunch 73
In Hindsight 87

INTRODUCTION

'There is no sophistry in my body: My manners are
tearing off heads,' says the hawk in Ted Hughes's poem,
'Hawk Roosting'.

Human beings are different: replete with sophistry, their
manners are the subject of weighty tomes and disquisitions. Manners are anatomised, prescribed and questioned. They were, thought Edmund Burke, more important than laws. They "vex or soothe, corrupt or purify, exalt or debase, barbarise or refine us, by a constant, steady, uniform, insensible operation, like that of the air we breathe in."

It is that insensible operation, in tune with sensibility, habit and orientation, that affects us so deeply yet subtly when we are removed from the familiar and enter the realm of the Brobdignagians, the Hyperborians or the inhabitants of the Devil's Head in the Valley Perilous, "beside that Isle of Mistorak" the 16th century English traveller, Sir John Mandeville wrote about. Strange, unbearably strange and dangerous.

It takes only a little to throw us off our balance: a little sadness, a little fear, a little temptation, and all the more so when we are disorientated to start with, when we cannot quite get our bearings. The concept of manners, in this sense, is not merely a matter of etiquette and procedure, though these come into it: it is meanings and interpretations. What to reply to X? How to approach Y? What to do in case of W? What in fact is that feeling we hardly noticed before but which we now seem to recognize in ourselves, and what to do with it? It hurts, it distresses, it jabbers away quietly in the background so we can't hear ourselves think. How vulnerable we suddenly are, not knowing what to do with that feeling, what to name it, how to address it!

Elizabeth MacDonald's stories are set in Italy but they all involve English, Irish or American professionals working and living in Italy. They are at home in their professional lives, but somewhat disorientated in their thoughts, feelings and social positions. Writing with great delicacy she watches her characters in the act of losing balance, tipping ever so slightly into what could be serious trouble. The stories are beautifully paced and cadenced, rejecting grand conclusions. They end on edge, not quite toppling, so no-one actually falls but we feel their vertigo and register it by the most refined, understated of means.

In musicians we talk of a marvellous ear, or perfect pitch. MacDonald's pitch is pretty marvellous. We are in the ancient city of Pisa where life goes on in the hallowed Tuscan manner: family, mama, beauty, spontaneity, hierarchy, a touch of old fashioned sexism. On the other hand no anglo-saxon starchiness, no booziness, no outright vulgarity or tight-assed squirming. At home each quality is familiar and neatly mapped: abroad the proportions change. They bulge and quiver and draw attention to themselves. The resident but retired art historian, embarrassed by a group of assorted Irish, English and American tourists, watches the English woman waltz off with the nearest flirt and pronounces the word 'plebeian'. In the company around the table there is, the story says, "an audible intake of breath" on which the professor reflects, "it's not the type of thing one likes to hear anyone coming out with, still less oneself". That is close to perfect pitch, as is the writing that has carried us to this point, slightly crusty, slightly pompous as voiced for the old man, but light as a feather in the mouth of the narrator behind him.

In Holbein's famous picture of *The Ambassadors* there is an equally famous detail, an anamorphic skull painted so that it can only be seen from an acute angle to the picture, not head on. From head on it is simply a vague shape we look beyond and ignore. The true writer, who is everywhere at home and nowhere at home, is always slightly at an angle to the picture, always looking for that anamorphic skull, even if only as a metaphor, because she knows that life contains such figures, such metaphors. The figure need not always be a skull of course: it could be a bouquet, a bottle of wine, indeed anything at all; it may simply be what Henry James called 'the figure in the carpet', nevertheless there is something ghostly and glimpsed about it. The writer senses the anamorphic presence and watches it appear at the core of her own writing, much as it had appeared to her in the picture of the world. There, she says. It's true.

The stories in this book are full of such figures and skulls. The world in which they appear is charming, appealing to the senses and the imagination, and the writer's eye lingers patiently over its details, patiently but warily looking for that figure, that skull, sensing its presence. Nothing much seems to happen but as we sit with her, slowly we too begin to sense the anamorphic figure in the foreground.

"There was a moment," the writer says in her Preface, "in which I stopped seeing the Italians as so many foreigners, and started seeing myself through their eyes: the solitary foreigner. Just what kind of a discovery was this? What kind of a Pandora's box did I open?"

But then she nips down to the fruit and vegetable market. She dons her sunglasses. Everywhere at home and nowhere at home: the fresh unfamiliar lightness and mystery of the world. The oddity of the world's manner of being. The location of the anamorphic skull beyond the dark glasses, glimpsed somewhere outside them, at a sharp angle, past the edge. The vertigo.

George Szirtes

PREFACE

From behind the glass partition of the counter, his fingers poised over the keyboard, the bank clerk doesn't even bother to look at me as he asks, "*Nome?*"

"Elizabeth MacDonald."

The grey head swivels towards me. "*Eh?!*" he erupts. His dark eyebrows bristle.

"Ey-leeds-ah-bett-ma-kah-daw-naald." I repeat, enunciating every syllable as if I were dealing with a five-year-old. It never fails.

"*Aaahhh.*" A long drawn-out syllable of dawning comprehension. The eyebrows lift. Then rapidly they descend again. "*Sì, sì, certo.*" He nods vigorously, and for the benefit of the lengthy queue behind me, adds in a loud voice, "*Comunque sapevo che era straniera, lei.*"

So you knew I was foreign all along? Yeah right, Luigi. That's not the impression you gave a moment ago when I read you my account number.

"*Sì, sì, certo,*" I echo, and then give him a cursory smile. Hopefully he will desist from any further useless exchanges. The queue, however, has other ideas: sensing drama in the offing – or at least a bit of gossip to bring home to the lunch-table – every pretence at orderly patience evaporates and they surge forward. Suddenly I am surrounded by a huddle of beady eyes that flick expectantly from my face to that of the clerk. Perspiration breaks out on my back. My overdraft will come to light – it will be writ large on his screen. Facts of a tawdry nature will be raked over for the edification of all.

The bank clerk and I have reversed roles. He now has assumed an air of joviality, fortified in the knowledge that things are once again back on a recognisable footing. My chin inches forward. He plays shamelessly to the gallery.

"*Ma-kah-daw-naald*?" He casts a complicit look around the assembled citizenry, before enquiring, "*Non sarà mica una di quelli degli hamburger?*"

'Aaam-boor-gherr. The citizenry titters appreciatively. Then falls silent, as their eyes slew back to me. *Non si sa mai* – I might actually be a part of the despised hamburger dynasty.

I glower at him. "*Come no*," I answer, thin-lipped, "*sono una parente povera.*"

A poor relation. The citizenry hesitates, not sure whether this is an instance of ready wit (unlikely in a foreigner), or the unsettling truth. A murmur builds up. They begin to debate the issue: comments on my appearance, clothes and manner are bandied back and forth with the efficacy of shuttlecocks aimed at a dartboard. The bank clerk observes the proceedings, an expression of detached smugness on his face. I battle with a rising tide of fury.

"*Signori!*" I expostulate, with all the rigid indignation of which I am capable (considerable at that point), "*Per cortesia, un po' di* privacy!" I give the last word an extra anglophone flourish.

"*Ehhh*?!"

"*Prrai-vah-see!*"

"*Aaahhh…*"

There is much shrugging. The crowd reluctantly disperses. It can't be a coincidence that there is no equivalent word in Italian for 'privacy'; the concept doesn't figure very high on their list of priorities. I turn a baleful eye on the instigator of my public embarrassment. He returns it with one of candid curiosity.

"*Americana?*" he ventures.

"*No.*"

"*Inglese?*"

"*No.*"

He scratches his neck, stumped. Then he slaps his hand down on the counter. "*Scozzese!*" he announces jubilantly.

"*No.*"

His shoulders sag.

"*Irlandese.*" I say, with grim satisfaction.

Try telling me you knew that already, Luigi.

"*Irlandese!*" His eyes light up. "*Che bel paese!*"

What a dastardly advantage. My righteous indignation begins to waver. It's hard to resist a compliment paid to one's far-off homeland. I muster up a semblance of a smile.

He prattles on in this fashion for the duration of the transaction: the wonderful holiday they'd had there two years ago; the sheep, the bogs, the hills; so quaint. All the drunks they'd seen! Not so sure about the rain, but what can you do? And do I spell Ey-leeds-ah-bett with an 's' or a 'z'?

"'Z'".

"*Beh, sì – è chiaro.*"

By the time we have concluded, his eyes are twinkling away at me.

"*Arrivederci, signora.*"

"*Arrivederci,*" I simper, and slink out.

In the open air, the sunlight spills out of a cloudless blue sky. There is a crystalline limpidity to the day that only materialises in late May or September; it washes over the façades of the *palazzi* around the *piazza*, intensifying the ochre of the plaster-work and the red of the bricks. The warm air wraps itself around me and brings with it the smoky-sweet scent of jasmine; up to my left, the balustrade of a terrace is barely visible under a tumbling mass of small white stars. It's half past ten on a Wednesday morning in early Summer, and the world has caught me by surprise.

This is bloody typical though. What was all that pantomime in aid of? Can this sort of thing be useful? What exactly would it change if I did spell my name with an 's' rather than a 'z'? After umpteen years living in Italy, have I still not fitted in enough? Have I fitted in too much? What is home anyway? The where and the what of home have split like mercury: they won't be pinned down and it's unlikely they'll ever come together again.

There was a moment – when was it? – in which I stopped seeing the Italians as so many foreigners, and started seeing myself through their eyes: the solitary foreigner. Just what kind of a discovery was this?

What kind of a Pandora's box did I open?

The sunlight dancing on the bare backs of my legs impinges. The fruit and vegetable market is just across the way; I need tomatoes, fresh basil and strawberries. I don my sunglasses.

NO MAN IS AN ISLAND

The whistling and blustering of the wind had penetrated the darkness of the room. Now it rattled at the edge of his consciousness, its moaning dragging him from a deep sleep. He heaved around grumpily in the bed and punched the pillow into a more amenable shape. And there it was again. That invisible surge pressing in on the shutters, then slackening its hold, a hoarse exhalation that fell abruptly into nothingness.

There must be a bloody awful storm out there. What time was it? The alarm clock beside his bed shone the time redly into the blackness: eleven forty-eight. Another late awakening. Groggily, he sat up on an elbow. There was silence in the apartment; the others had long gone out, he guessed. A jaw-cracker of a yawn, and then he steeled himself to get out from under the warmth of the duvet. The window was nearer than the light switch over by the door. A tentative toe on the cold terracotta surface of the floor failed to meet either of his runners, so he hopped barefoot over towards the window. An icy shaft of air hissing in through the cracks in the window frame sliced his face. He fumbled with the catch of the white inner shutters, *gli scuri*, and threw them back. Next he opened the windows, and then finally put his hand to the catch of the green slatted outer shutters, *le persiane*. The force of the wind was such that he could not immediately push them open. Suddenly they were whipped out of his hold, and slammed against the outside wall with a crash. He leaned hurriedly out of the large window to secure them in their rusty iron catches; the impact had flaked off some more of the ochre-coloured plaster covering the building.

And then it struck him. Bright sunlight and a strip of clear blue sky visible between the two tall rows of old *palazzi* lining Via della Faggiola. What a strange day. Not at all what he had been expecting. Up high, a small cloud gusted headlong from one side of the narrow strip to the other like golden-white tumbleweed, its edges fraying under the invisible hooks of the harrying wind.

⸎

He glanced around the sparsely furnished kitchen. The shutters had been opened on the curtainless window, but the table was bare. Lorenzo and Rocco had probably had their coffee and *cornetto* at the *bar* just down the road. The *bar* provided free copies of the *Gazzetta dello sport,* and they both liked their football.

The dishes from last night's dinner were still piled up in the large ceramic sink: it was his turn to wash them, but he didn't feel like doing that now. They'd have to wait till he got back from teaching in the evening.

Six hours of English lessons lay ahead of him that after-noon, half-two to half-eight, non-stop teaching, and all he wanted to do was relax quietly until it was time to set off for the school. The mocha coffee pot hung unused from the metal dish rack over the sink, so he took it down, filled it, and placed it on a low heat on the rudimentary stove.

But what was there to eat? He hadn't managed to do a shopping yesterday. If there was some bread left over from last night's dinner, he could heat it up in the oven. Not for the first time he wished he'd got round to buying a toaster. He went to check if there was any butter and jam left in the fridge. As he opened it, his eye fell on the yellow post-it on the door. Rocco suggesting the three of them have a game of Risiko that evening after dinner. Well, fine. He'd no unpostponable plans one way or another.

Risiko. The game was mildly entertaining, although by the end of the evening he knew he'd be as worked up about winning as the other two. Except that he'd be the one trying to hide it. He could just see it: Lorenzo cursing in a stream of those anti-religious *bestemmie* that Tuscans set such store by, Rocco languishing melodramatically, and himself fuming silently. Rocco and he were like chalk and cheese: appearance, mentality, background, everything. How had he come to be living with such a guy?

Well, the guy had come to the school looking for private lessons. Rocco had needed help in translating a load of articles in English that were crucial for the completion of his massive thesis in archaeology, and he was the only teacher in the school who had been qualified enough to take him on. The so-called advantages of a Classics degree... And then without really knowing anything about him, except that he had a good Classics education and was a native speaker of English, Rocco had seemed to take him under his wing. He found himself invited out and about around Pisa, introduced to an endless circle of student friends, exhibited as somewhat of an exotic catch. Although, maybe he was being just a bit thin-skinned there.

But that was when he had begun to notice that Rocco always spoke to him in English. He grimaced. Rocco had brought all the fervour of a convert to the linguistic enterprise, proof of this being his suggestion that they find a place to live together: that way Rocco could, as he put it, make the most of the opportunity to practise his English out-of-hours. Though the overtone of the word he'd used, *approfittare*, sounded closer to 'exploit'. Rocco hadn't seemed to give a thought to the fact that this was scuppering his own attempts to learn Italian. Nor had Rocco been bothered by scruples that he might want to switch out of teaching mode for the few hours he had free from the school. In the grand scheme of things, learning English was just more important than learning Italian: one was a necessity, the other an indulgence.

Rocco's suggestion had, nevertheless, been timely. The contract in his old apartment had been due to expire, and he was dying to get out of it. He'd had the only single room in an apartment of shared double rooms. Nominally, the total number of occupants was seven, but this didn't allow for girlfriends staying over, friends dropping by, and – not infrequently – the landlady herself appearing out of nowhere, to ensure that decorum was being observed. On these occasions, girlfriends and male friends were shoved promiscuously into wardrobes, presses and broom cupboards.

He couldn't get over the hypocrisy of it. They were all adults in their twenties, for Christ's sake. What was the problem? And why was everyone so okay with having to pay lip service to this charade? Basically, even though only a couple of years separated them, they were living in two different worlds: he had cut the ties with the student lifestyle and was working, while they were still leading a carefree student existence.

Time to move on. The low rent was no compensation for that kind of daily farce. He still couldn't afford to live on his own, but if he could find some post-graduate student nearer his own age to move in with, things might take a turn for the better. That was when Rocco had come up with the suggestion of a third person in the apartment; it had not

4

been to his liking. But when he met Lorenzo, saw the size of the apartment, and realised that each of them would have their own room, he'd changed his mind. He got on okay with Lorenzo, who was doing post-grad archaeology with Rocco, and kept pretty much to himself. And because the apartment was mouldering away on the top floor of an old building in an advanced state of disrepair, the rent was reasonable too. Plus, he liked living in the centre of Pisa, in one of the historic streets – even if it was a bit rundown.

Rocco was going out with a girl from his own village down south. They had been going out since their last year of high school, which amounted to a whopping eight years at this stage. But she never stayed over. She was a boarder in the convent further up the road and had a curfew at ten. Except on Saturday night, when she could enjoy the electrifying experience of staying out until midnight.

What was that about? What kind of a medieval arrangement was that? Especially as the two of them spent marathon sessions locked away in Rocco's room, only to scoot out the door at ten to ten, so as to have her deposited safely back in the nunnery on the dot of ten. One evening, as the three of them were gathered around the kitchen table, he had asked Rocco why he was a party to such tomfoolery. Rocco had shrugged slowly and expressively, his upturned hands contriving to communicate both bafflement and sagacity. He remained silent as Imma placed his dish of pasta in front of him, his eyes focused reflectively on some distant point of the opposite wall. Rocco and Imma always had meals at home, as they were deeply suspicious of the standards of hygiene of anything they had not made themselves.

"It's something you just wouldn't understand," Rocco said eventually, and took a forkful of pasta. "It's the easiest way to keep everyone happy."

Imma placed a dish of pasta in front of him as well, and then sat down to her own. He was caught between gratefulness at his hunger pangs being met, and distaste at the suspicion that he was being mothered. "But what about keeping yourselves happy?" he pursued. "How happy are you with this arrangement?"

"Listen, Steven," said Rocco, laying his fork down. "It's not as black and white as that. It's not just a question of how happy the two of us are. We come from large extended families who live in a small village. Like your poet says, 'No man is an island,' no?"

"But you're here!" exclaimed Steven. "Who's going to be any the wiser?"

Rocco's head moved rhythmically from side to side, his expression switching to regretful scepticism. "Unfortunately, not so true. Imma's second cousin stays at the convent too, so it would get back to her parents immediately if she did anything wild." He turned to Imma and added, "And we don't want that. Imma and her family are *brava gente, gente per bene.*"

Imma smiled complacently. After all, one could never be considered too respectable.

A frown then settled on his features as he observed Steven. "You're the person with all the freedom," he said, folding his arms. "You're the one on your own in a foreign country. You've no-one to look out for you." He pushed his glasses more firmly onto the bridge of his nose. "But no-one – how do you say? – checking you up either." He took up his fork again and applied himself silently to the rest of his pasta.

Steven had already wolfed his down. It came to him that he and Rocco were equally suspicious of each other. But, of the two of them, it was the person mired in family ties who was in reality having all the fun. All his glorious freedom seemed to have amounted to was this solitude. As the pair of them hadn't scrupled to hint to him on occasion, maybe he *was* just a sad case.

∽

He banged the large door behind him. Across the street, the fluffy yellow blossoms of a mimosa tree shivered on the branches trailing down over a high garden wall. Only the top half of the tree was visible. The branches reeled in the streaming wind, and the scent was an invisible dew in the cold golden-blue air. There was something giddy, unruly, about this strange day that unsettled him, made him loath to shut himself away in the classroom. Last year he'd taken off with a group of student friends to enjoy the carnival in Viareggio. This year he couldn't.

A vague feeling of disquiet took hold of him. And then, unexpectedly, the sight of the mimosa tree and all its vulnerable little blossoms irritated him.

Well, if even the mimosa was irritating him now, things were not looking good. Good will was in very short supply. And yet he'd been so full of it setting out, in search of a more genuine way of life, closer to – closer to what? He couldn't say. It was just a lack that he was aware of, rather than understood. Although, he did know what he was getting away from: the strait-jacket impositions of society at home.

But, as he was finding to his cost, there was no end to the impositions to be understood and the strait-jackets to be worn.

Even worse, the precise nature of the strait-jacket poised to smother him in Italy still eluded him. All he had to go on was a creeping sense of distaste for something amorphous that made him want to buck leap around the place from time to time.

And what was so genuine about slaving to pay the bills? Or maybe it was indeed all too genuine.

What was he doing here? Somewhere down the line, his delight and openness to diversity had transmuted into constant low-key pain and regret, an abiding sense of loss. How had that happened? He no longer felt in control of his life and it wasn't a pleasant sensation.

He shook his head impatiently. This strange day, this strange hybrid day – wild wind and cold sunshine – was stirring up something he couldn't put a name on.

Did his reason for staying here – like all seasoned ex-pats – boil down to the weather? It was only February, and here was Spring on the way. There indeed he was obviously onto a winner. Obviously.

Out on Borgo Stretto, the *pasticcerie* windows were full of carnival-time cakes. *Zeppole, frittelle di riso, cenci.* No time to stop and buy some now, otherwise he'd be late. The street, littered with *coriandoli* and streamers, rang with the excited cries of small children rigged out in costumes. Maybe he should phone in sick or something, and take off for the afternoon. Who could tell when there'd be a day like this again. But with his luck, he'd get caught. He knew he just wouldn't have the neck to come up with a suitably bare-faced lie and get himself out of trouble. And, unlike Rocco and Imma, whose fond parents paid for everything, he had to take care of his own bills.

❧

The muted tones of Lorenzo's deep voice reverberated down through the dank air of the dimly lit stairwell to where Steven was, on the second floor. He smiled to himself as he made his way up the last flight of stairs, listening to the burst of laughter that reached the landing. He turned the key in the latch and walked in; his face tingled in the sudden rush of warm air and his coat smelt of the freezing air outside as he hung it up. Lorenzo was standing in the middle of the kitchen telling a story, the light from the bare bulb falling on his head. He drew up a chair to the table, noting that it was already set for dinner, and listened with pleasure to the crisp, aspirated sounds of Lorenzo's Tuscan delivery. But he didn't manage to catch everything and so could only smile ruefully when the other two started to laugh at the conclusion of the story.

"*Uè*," said Rocco, turning to him. "*È arrivato l'imboscato!*"

"The what's arrived?"

"*L'imboscato*. The, the –" Rocco screwed up his face in concentration. "The shirker. You can say shirker, can't you?"

"Yeah, you can. But you may not. Now there's a useful lesson for you in English. Why would you want to say 'shirker'? I've just knocked off after six hours' teaching."

Rocco sighed at length. He pointed in the direction of the sink. It was empty. "It was your turn to do the dishes. It took Lorenzo forty-five minutes to get through that lot."

"Oh, right. The dishes. Sorry about that."

"You know, maybe it doesn't upset you to be in a room with dirty dishes, but it upsets me. There isn't another room to relax in, so the least we can do is keep this one tidy."

"Okay, okay. I get your point." This was beginning to piss him off.

"We're not used to such an unhygienic approach to the home."

That was just one step too far. He chewed his bottom lip for a moment, and then looked Rocco in the eyes. "But who gives a shit about outside the home, right?"

"Eh?"

Steven tapped the plastic tablecloth. It, um, upsets me to see you cleaning this by shaking it out the window. Just about ruins my day. To say nothing about the poor suckers passing below. And what's with the sacks of rubbish left rotting out on the landing? Are you waiting to see if the good fairy will come along and magic them away?"

"Look," interjected Lorenzo, "how about we fix this misunderstanding, and then let it go?"

"Suits me," said Steven.

"Everyone has a task to do," continued Lorenzo. "You miss your turn this time, you do double next time. Okay?"

"Sounds fair enough."

⸎

The dice clattered across the board. A one and a three. Rocco groaned and threw his hands in the air. "*Ma che palle turche*! *Che rogna*! *Che* – "

"*Sfiga*!" finished up Lorenzo. "*Sei proprio un povero sfigato*." He chuckled and turned to Steven. "Lady Luck's spitting in his eye this evening, eh?"

Steven sniggered.

"Laugh, laugh all you like," said Rocco, yawning. "But you know how the saying goes: lucky at the gaming table, unlucky in love. Now who are the real losers?" He got up. "I'm making myself some more coffee. You want some?"

"No, thanks."

"Another beer?" Lorenzo held out a bottle to Steven.

"Another one!" Rocco snorted incredulously. "This'll be your fourth!"

Steven sat back from the table and folded his arms. "It's unbelievable," he said, looking at Lorenzo. "It's worse than living with my mother."

"*Ah, la mamma...*" replied Rocco. "And did you leave all your dirty dishes for her to clean up as well?"

"*E dacci un taglio, te, che sei pesante*," Lorenzo shot at Rocco.

Rocco's mouth opened and then shut; instead, his eyebrows arched and he pushed his glasses back up onto the bridge of his nose.

A muscle in Steven' jaw was twitching. "Yeah, Lorenzo's right. Knock it off – you really are heavy going. But here's a new word for you, Rocco." He paused, and then added very quietly, "Ever heard of 'sissy'?"

Rocco looked at him interrogatively.

"That's what we call guys who are still calling their mothers 'Mama' long after its sell-by date."

"Is for all Italians, then!" laughed Lorenzo.

Steven took a swig out of the bottle of beer Lorenzo had opened for him. "No offence or anything, but it makes me really queasy to hear any Italian over the age of seven call his mother '*mamma*'."

"No offence taken," said Rocco, coming back over to the table and sitting down. "Sorry I give you a hard time. Take it as a compliment. If I am not so interested in your language and culture, I don't spend so much time trying to figure it out." He shrugged. "But it's not easy." He smiled slowly. "Sissy, eh?"

"It's not easy even for us Italians," added Lorenzo. "I mean, there are big differences between Italians from the South, from the Centre, and from the North. We don't always – how can I say? – appreciate one another."

"And that's only among yourselves," said Steven.

"But," Rocco shook his head, "no matter how much I admire the Anglo-Saxon language and culture, I find it cold. Inhospitable."

"What?" exclaimed Steven. "I suppose this is part of the 've-got-all-the-monopoly-on-emotion' thing you keep banging on about."

"*Beh, un po' rigidino lo sei,*" said Lorenzo.

"He says you're a bit stiff," supplied Rocco obligingly. "I think you're a bit cold," he added. "But I admire you for it. It's the famous self-control, I suppose."

"Well, there you go." Steven fell silent.

"But, you have said something very important," said Rocco. He paused. "The whole *mamma* thing – is the key to this big difference I feel between you and me. Bridging this –" His index finger and thumb pointed like a pistol, he rapidly shook the hand from side to side, " – is impossible!"

"Southerners," Lorenzo said confidentially to Steven, "love philosophizing about life. We Tuscans get on with living it." He took a slug out of his bottle, and belched quietly.

Rocco extended his arms, a pained expression on his face. "You know, you Tuscans really are vulgar."

Steven had to laugh: he loved the way all Italians bandied this word around, without even a hint of apology and impervious to all taint of snobbery.

Rocco brought his hands together, joining the finger-tips, which he drummed meditatively. "How, for instance, would you say '*oh madonna*'?"

"Well, I suppose you'd have to change it a bit," replied Steven, "and so, probably, 'Oh my God!'"

"And what about '*Mamma mia*!'"

"Yeah – that you'd definitely have to change." Steven considered for a moment. "Maybe something nice and safely abstract like, 'Goodness me!', or 'My word!'. Or even, 'Oh boy!', or 'Oh man!'"

The three of them looked at each other for a moment, and then smiled.

"No," said Rocco, shaking his head. "English doesn't feel like a language I could be at home in. I wouldn't feel like I intimately belonged."

"So now you see!" cried Lorenzo, raising his beer bottle in a toast. "The one thing that unites all Italians, South, Centre, and North, is reverence for '*la mamma*'."

"Just so long as it's not catching…" said Steven, looking away.

It was the silence that woke him. So dense as to feel like a physical presence. His eyes flew to the clock, but it was only nine. Cautiously, he got up and made his way to the window. As soon as he opened the *scuri*, a strange milky white glow poured into the room. He opened the windows and threw back the shutters.

Wrong-footed again.

From a pewter sky, snow flakes came falling dreamily through the silent air. Into the hushed stillness, the flakes unceasingly spiralled. Such a uniform covering from such random descent. The green slats of the shutters; the red tiles of the roofs; the black surface of the road; the yellow of the mimosa: all transfigured by this shimmering veneer of white. And all around him that uncanny silence, as muffling as an icy blanket.

What did they mean rigid, cold? It wasn't he who was cold. This was cold. Unexpectedly cold.

WISTERIA

A swift spiralled by Ann, calling shrilly in the evening air. She walked over to the railings surrounding the top-floor terrace of the hotel, and her eye roamed out over the city spread below her. A jumble of narrow winding streets, red roofs, green shutters, ochre coloured buildings and church spires. The streetlamps were just beginning to come on, their meandering lines dotting the city, and her eye followed them as they glimmered here and there, out as far as the indigo mountains that circled the city to the north. The *Monti Pisani*.

It was a spring evening in late April, and the sun was setting, hovering just above the horizon in a haze of pulsating crimson and gold. Set against it, the famous, tilted tower was like a ship going down in a storm, a luminous white mast tossed in a sea of liquid fire.

Ann jumped as another swift shot past her, so close that she could see its beak, calling out to the other darting birds as they swooped and circled through the air in a frenetic quest for insects before night fell. The very air, cut into fleeting wisps of speed by the swifts, seemed to teeter on the brink of a vortex of madness.

She turned away from the railings to watch the white-coated waiters as they moved deftly among the orchestra members who were converging under a large pergola. The pergola was spectacular, laden with bauble after bauble of frothy wisteria. Even at this remove the scent was weaving lilac ribbons of smoky sweetness around her. To the east the sky had turned a peacock blue, in which a few points of silver had begun to flicker. She breathed in deeply. How could she have forgotten the vulnerable intensity of an Italian spring evening?

She moved over to find out what the waiters were serving. More joy. There on a table were several bowls of the season's first strawberries. A waiter handed her a glass of *prosecco*. She picked out a strawberry, held it against the last traces of red in the sky, bit into its juicy ripeness, and relished the bubbles of *prosecco* breaking against her palate. Who would want to be anywhere else?

An expectant hush fell over the assembled orchestra players as her husband Charles joined them all on the terrace. At fifty-eight, he was still an imposing figure: tall, trim, his still thick, now white hair brushed back from his face. He walked over to her and, sliding his hand under her elbow, gave her a kiss on the cheek.

The leader of the orchestra moved over beside them and engaged Charles in conversation. Ann watched her husband as he spoke, noting his easy affableness. She knew that he was relishing the prospect of this tour around Tuscany.

Then Contessa Fiammetta Contini Della Quercia walked purposefully out onto the terrace, looked to right and left, saw Charles, and made straight for him. She gave him her hand and smiled; he raised it to his lips and said all that was proper. Ann was glad she'd made the effort to get her hair done that afternoon.

"It's such a pleasure to see you again," said the Contessa, smiling at Ann and inclining her head.

"Well, it's certainly a pleasure to be here again, Contessa," replied Ann.

"Oh, please – call me Fiammetta!" exclaimed the Contessa. "Charles already does…"

A waiter scurried over with some *prosecco*, and then Charles called for silence.

"Let us raise our glasses to the Contessa," he said. "For the unstinting generosity she has shown in helping to organise this whole venture. *Salute!*"

Everyone dutifully raised a glass.

The Contessa moved forward. "Ladies and gentlemen," she said smoothly, "On behalf of the committee of *Primavera Pisana,* I am delighted to welcome you to the city. We feel sure that this venture will become a yearly appointment for music lovers from Tuscany, and indeed further afield, and hope that you enjoy your stay here."

Everyone smiled, and Charles and the Contessa then fell into conversation.

Yes, thought Ann, she really spoke excellent English. Came from one of those noble families where they were as comfortable in German and English as they were in Italian. She moved back over to the railings and observed Charles and Fiammetta from her vantage point. Fiammetta certainly was a remarkable woman, possessed of a natural *hauteur* which her imposing height underlined. Indeed, in her shoes she was as tall as Charles. Ann guessed that she was in or about the same age as herself, but as far as individual style was concerned, they couldn't have been more different. Anne favoured a classic look: simple lines, understated colours, and under no circumstances, anything that had even a whiff of mutton-dressed-as-lamb. Fiammetta was attired in the latest fashion, obviously designer-label. In

Anne's world a thirty year old would have trouble carrying off that body-hugging apricot jersey dress which fell appreciably short of the knee. Of course, it helped that her legs were tanned and toned, and set off by a pair of high court shoes in beautiful leather.

Last September the two women had met for the first time. The experience was still very vivid in Ann's mind. Uncomfortably so, she now reflected, glancing over at Fiammetta once again. She had been over for a conference on Verdi and the Italian *Risorgimento* organised by the University, and a concert was offered on one of the evenings. That was where she had met Fiammetta, whose son was the pianist in a duo playing a selection of Brahms sonatas for violin and piano. They were introduced after the concert, and in the course of the conversation Ann's escort had told Fiammetta that Ann was married to Charles Boylan, the conductor.

A glitter had shot through Fiammetta's eyes at this news. Her hitherto perfunctory manner became attentive, and Ann had the unsettling sensation of two very pale blue eyes being suddenly brought to bear on her with penetrating intensity.

"And is your interest in music more amateurish?" she enquired, one eyebrow raised expectantly.

Ann bristled at this. "It depends what you mean by amateurish," she replied. "I'm a qualified music teacher, but I'm not teaching at the moment. And you?"

"Oh, I certainly don't teach music," Fiammetta laughed. "But I do know how to recognise talent when I hear it. As you must…" She smiled slowly at Ann; the smile didn't reach her extraordinary eyes, which continued to regard Ann speculatively. Then she added, "So what did you think of my son Federico?"

Ann was taken aback, but relieved that at least she could be sincere in her praise. Fiammetta listened closely. "I would like you to meet Federico," she said to Ann, "Why don't we go to his dressing room?"

As if at an unspoken command, the mass of people in the foyer of the theatre drew apart to let the Contessa pass. Ann, who was following in her wake, noted the surreptitious, but keen, glances that were cast after her.

Fiammetta rapped peremptorily on the door of the dressing room, and without waiting for an answer, sailed in.

"Oh, I –" faltered Ann. Federico was standing in front of the mirror combing his hair, clad only in a pair of very succinct and colourful underpants. "I think I should come back at a more suitable moment." She began to back out the door.

"Nonsense," said Fiammetta, shrugging dismissively. "Have you never seen a man before?" She made a sharp downward movement with the splayed fingers of her hand, indicating that Ann move closer. Then she turned to her son.

"*Bravo, bravissimo!*" she cried, taking his face in her hands. "My darling, you were just sublime." She ran a hand through his hair, ruffling it. "But you know, my love, that I prefer you with no gel in your hair." She caught him playfully by the chin and tweaked it, her bracelets jangling. "I want you to meet Ann Boylan, wife of Charles Boylan." She looked at him for a long moment, a smile flitting over her lips.

Ann shook hands with Federico, complimenting him on his performance. He had his mother's eyes. She had lots of time to observe them, as she was damned if she was looking anywhere else. Mother and son were indeed very similar, both tall, with dark blond hair, and olive complexions in which the ice-shot blueness of their eyes stood out. There was a pause, and then Federico said, "Well, if you'll excuse me, I'm getting dressed and going next door to Roberto." He quickly got into a pair of trousers and a jumper and headed for the door.

"*Ciao, tesoro*," Fiammetta called after him, and turning to Ann added, "They make a wonderful pair, Federico and Roberto – such wonderful empathy in their playing."

With determined charm, Fiammetta then steered the conversation round to the possibility of inviting Charles over to Tuscany for a series of concerts; if Charles should want to include a piano concerto in his programme, so much the better. And might she put Federico's name forward as soloist?

"I'll give you a recording you can take back to the Maestro," she concluded, "That way he'll be able to judge for himself."

Ann got back to her group of colleagues and was glad to hear they were moving on for something to eat in a little restaurant just beside the theatre. She felt as though she'd been standing in a gale force wind for the past half-hour. And now with the sudden disappearance of the wind, she found herself next to keeling over, unaware of just how much she'd been straining into it.

As they ate their delicious *antipasti*, the Italian colleague to her left asked if she knew the Contessa.

"No, I'd never met her before," replied Ann.

"A formidable woman, isn't she?"

"Oh, indeed."

"Considering she's been through so much," he added, pausing to shake his head sorrowfully before popping the contents of his fork into his mouth with relish.

"Oh?" prompted Ann, trying to keep the curiosity in her voice down to acceptable levels.

"Oh, yes," took up her colleague, "her husband, the Conte, ran off with the Austrian au pair twenty years ago, leaving Fiammetta with Federico, who was just four. Ludovico and the au pair disappeared to Argentina, where they've been living ever since. Fiammetta never re-married,"

his eyes briefly caught those of Ann, "for whatever reason…
And since then she's been living alone in the villa with her
Federico. Such a terrible humiliation for poor Fiammetta,"
he concluded, chewing happily on his *bresaola*.

So she'd taken the recording back to Charles and he'd
listened to it. Then he'd examined Federico's CV, and
pronounced that there was a definite talent there.
Fiammetta was contacted and the organisation of the tour
got under way.

And here they were, the night before their first concert,
which was to take place in Fiammetta's sumptuous villa in
the hills between Pisa and Lucca. It was to be a gala
evening, and the tickets had all sold out. Charles would
then take the concert on to Fiesole, Siena and Arezzo,
before winding up in the Teatro Verdi in Pisa.

She was shaken from her reverie by Fiammetta's voice.

"*Cara*, you were a million miles away," she said.

"Indeed," replied Ann. "It's such a beautiful evening –
I'm just making the most of it."

"Of course. After all, you'll be back to your rain and fog
soon enough." Fiammetta smiled briefly and then
announced, "My ex-husband will be arriving for the
concert tomorrow. I wrote to tell him about Federico's
achievement – I bear the man no ill will – and it's only right
he should know."

"Arriving from where?" Ann asked innocently, enjoying
the unexpected glut of information.

"From Argentina," replied Fiammetta. "I haven't seen
him these twenty years. He's an elderly man at this stage –"
She paused to consider, the faintest hint of a smile indicating a malevolent enjoyment of this fact. "Yes, he's all of
seventy now. And of course, he never managed to have any
children with that other woman." A harsh rigidity suddenly
paralysed her face, giving it a clay-like brittleness which, in

the blue half-light of the terrace, seemed like a mask. "So now he's sentimental about the idea of a son. Federico is the only one he's got. The one who'll have to carry on the name." She looked away.

"I'm sure he'll be very proud," Ann murmured.

Fiammetta turned back to look her in the face. One side of her mouth twitched slightly; it was difficult to say whether in a smile or in scorn. Without saying a word, she moved off.

❧

The evening sunshine slanted in over the oval driveway that extended from the wrought-iron gateway up to the steps of the villa. As the car crunched over the gravel of the left side, Ann admired the beautifully tended lawn in the centre. To the right and left, evergreen trees of immense height formed an impenetrable frame around the villa and its driveway. Charles had just turned in off a busy road, and yet the frenetic reality of speeding cars and noise seemed to have fallen away into a void. It was an oasis of timelessness scooped out of the surrounding hills, in which a brooding introspection held the encroaching outside world at a distance.

They pulled up in front of the villa and got out of the car. They were in plenty of time. Ann shook out her dress and smoothed the creases. Charles took his bagged suit from the back of the car where it had been hanging: he would get changed later. She smiled at him.

"Quite a pile, isn't it?" he remarked, over the roof of the car.

"It certainly is," she replied.

The villa dated back to the sixteenth century. It loomed up out of the backdrop of greenery with a sombre bulk that lent it a fortress-like air. The main entrance was impressive:

a wide set of granite steps led up to the door, made of two enormously thick black panels of wood studded with giant-sized nails, on each of which rested a large wrought-iron knocker. One of these panels was now drawn back to reveal a red-jacketed manservant who welcomed them and ushered them in.

The golden brilliance of the evening sunshine was dissipated in the chilly gloom of the atrium. Ann's eyes adjusted to it, and were then drawn to a massive chandelier made of some dark material that could have been gilt-covered wood or time-darkened brass. It was suspended on a long chain and candles had been placed in all of its holders. They walked across the old terracotta flagging and were led into a room to the left. It was large and spacious, and here too a chandelier hung from its high timbered ceiling. The walls were covered in what Anne could only assume were original tapestries.

Fiammetta swept into the room in full evening regalia.

"*Carissimi,*" she cried, extending her hands in an embrace that stopped just short of actual contact, hovering near their shoulders, "I hope you had no trouble finding the villa?"

"None at all," replied Charles.

"Splendid," said Fiammetta. "Go on up to the first floor – we're using the principal *salone* there – and you can tell me if there's anything not to your liking, Charles."

"I'm sure there won't be," said Charles gallantly. "I just need to test the acoustic."

Fiammetta nodded. "And you, Ann," she added, her eyes flicking over Ann's gown, "I'm sure you won't object to being left on your own for a while – take a look around the villa – go wherever you please. I have some things to take care of for the reception afterwards. Besides which, my ex-husband will be arriving soon, and that will take up still more of my time." With a rustle of silk, she then headed over to the door. As Charles and Ann filed past her, she added, "It's *so* difficult to find decent servants these days. One has to oversee everything, down to the smallest details, otherwise they rob you blind. *Non c'é piú religione…*"

Ann was just as glad to be left on her own. It was one thing having to listen to Fiammetta when the mood took her to reveal some interesting little detail about her private life; it was quite another to have to listen to her complaining about the lack of a ready supply of serfs. She left Fiammetta to sort out the servants and followed Charles up to the *salone* on the first floor.

There were two high casement windows, beyond which she could see a soft evening radiance. She opened one of them and found that it led out onto a flag-stoned terrace which ran the length of the *salone*. There was a balustrade of great beauty around the terrace, on which terracotta vases full of trailing blue lobelia were placed. Spindly pale yellow blooms of freesia reached up out of vases on the ground towards the blue, creating a scented screen that picked up the colours in the sky of approaching twilight. She walked over to the balustrade and looked down and out over the land that stretched away in a gentle slope, up towards the surrounding hills. Olive trees interlaced with the white of apple and cherry blossom in an undulating dappled haze. She turned around to look back at the building, and over on the right-hand corner saw a magnificent display of wisteria. The second in as many days. It arched up over the far window, framing it in a rampant display of tenacious opulence, and Ann envied the lucky person who slept there. No wonder Italians called their own country *il Bel Paese*; it was indeed, and to an extent that bewildered.

How very strange though – keeping this area of beauty so private, to the back of the villa. No such thing as keeping the best side out. The important thing was to keep every one else out. The whole concept of the patio, within the house, which only its inhabitants could enjoy. Who knows – maybe for that reason they enjoyed it even more…

From within the *salone* a long solitary 'A' was sounded. Then the purposeful cacophony of an orchestra tuning up spilled out onto the terrace. It never failed to send a thrill of expectation shooting through Ann. She listened intently as Charles took up from the recapitulation of the first movement of Schubert's 5th Symphony. Despite the wooden-beamed ceiling, the acoustic was satisfactory and the music had a pleasing resonance to it. She relaxed.

Preparations for the reception afterwards were rapidly being completed by an army of servants. Suddenly their voices faded, and Ann turned to see Fiammetta coming out through the casement window. She minutely inspected the proceedings, reprimanded one of the menservants for having forgotten some napkins, and then turned to Ann. "It's time, *cara*," she said, "people are arriving and the concert will be starting shortly. Why don't you go in and take your seat?"

The concert was opening with Federico playing Ravel's concerto in G major. Ann was always nervous before any concert conducted by Charles. Indeed, she was often more nervous than he was, and for that reason kept away from him in case she communicated her malaise. But from the first notes, she knew that the performance would be top class. And the second movement, which was one of her favourite pieces of music, was eerily touching as its notes dropped like lunar pearls into the candlelit silence of the *salone*. Federico played well, and deserved his applause.

Ann linked her arm through Charles' as they walked out onto the terrace. It too was now candlelit.

"Well done, pet!" she beamed at him.

"So you think it went well, then?" asked Charles. But she could see that he was aware it had gone as he hoped.

"Up to your usual exacting standard," said Ann, giving his arm a squeeze.

All around them there was a buzz of conversation as the audience mixed with orchestra players, and various people came over to offer their congratulations. Federico appeared, with Roberto the violinist, and they helped themselves to glasses before approaching Charles.

"I'd just like to thank you for giving me the opportunity to perform with you," said Federico, "It was a great experience."

"Likewise for myself – you have a remarkable talent, and I'm sure it'll be the first of many important engagements." replied Charles. Federico turned and smiled happily at Roberto. Ann could see that he was on a high, and her heart warmed to his youthful hope and exuberance.

"Ah, there's your mother," she said, looking over at the window. Federico looked over as well.

"Yes," he said, his face darkening, "with my father." A glance passed between himself and Roberto. "If you'll excuse me," he said abruptly to Ann and Charles. "*Vieni, Roberto,*" and they were gone.

Ann watched with interest as he headed over to where his mother was standing with an elderly man. There was a slight lull in the rumble of conversation. Everyone here must realise that the old Conte had come back for the first time in twenty years to see his son and rejoice in his moment of triumph. There was no sign of the Austrian ex-au pair. Somebody behind Ann laughed softly.

Fiammetta, Federico, Roberto and the Conte were gathered in front of a tall cast-iron torch-holder, which flickered in the night breeze. They were like players in a Greek tragedy surrounded by a whispering chorus. Fiammetta's face had assumed that mask-like quality of the previous evening, and there was some immense rigidity in her demeanour that hinted at a welter of emotion kept barely under control. She was staring at her ex-husband as the old man congratulated his son, his arm clutching the young man's shoulder.

Then she moved forward and introduced Roberto. The expression on the old man's face froze, and he looked first at her, then at Federico, and finally at Roberto. His arm fell from Federico's shoulder. Federico put his arm around Roberto's. The old man stood stock still, as if paralysed. Silence fell; there was a long moment that dilated unbearably. And then suddenly the Conte turned and walked back into the *salone*.

Chatter resumed, glasses clinked, and glances were shooting around the terrace like spores from a dandelion after a gust of wind.

A waiter bearing glasses of *prosecco* passed by in front of the Contessa; she stopped him and took one. From under their heavy lids, her eyes glittered in the guttering light of the torch as they came to rest on Ann and Charles. Slowly, she lifted her glass and inclined her head.

FIREWORKS

"Helen – I'm just going out for a quick look around."

"Oh. Do you want to wait for me? I'll only take a minute to get dressed."

"Ah no, no. Don't bother getting up. I'll see you back here in an hour for dinner, all right?"

The door of the hotel room clicks after him. She lies back down in the bed and pulls the sheet up under her chin. Her eyes latch onto the closed door in the semi-darkness; its impassive solidity and the silence in the room suddenly become a scream in her head. Where is he off to in the rain, for God's sake?

It takes her a moment or two to register that the dull rumble of the downpour has actually stopped. Rain is the last thing she would have expected in Pisa in mid June. Bit of a disappointment, really, walking across the hotel room to close the dark green shutters against the deluge of oversize drops pelting off the sill. And then the gleam of greenish light rippling down over the impersonal white walls, its muted light expanding silkenly through the room like high-tide in an underwater grotto. From behind the slatted shutters, the acrid smell of rainwater on parched concrete and the riotous gurgling of flooded gutters tumbling down into the drains. Closed shutters and open windows in this enveloping warm air, protecting her rather than cutting her off from the outside world.

The strange intimacy of a hotel room on a rainy afternoon has touched her far more than bright sunshine would have, leaving her with a lingering sense of vulnerability. She tears the sheet off and gets up from the bed – the bed where they made love just an hour ago. And already she is assailed by the familiar churnings of anger. She removes the crumpled dress from the chair beside the bed and lets it slide over her sticky body. Then she walks over to the window and pushes back the shutters, dislodging a drop of water which splashes onto the warm bare skin of her arm; the shock makes her shiver slightly. Spread before her is a panoramic view of the city rooftops in the opaque evening light; oppressiveness is rolling through the sultry air in languorous waves. Below a mass of compacted inky clouds, a long strip of sky remains visible, sluiced with the streaming colours of a stormy sunset. Thunder rumbles in the distance, rattling through the heavy stillness of the air. In an inversion of a fireworks display, a flock of starlings billows across the sulphurous expanse of sky, mushrooming darkly against the seared brilliance before contracting and then falling apart.

Helen looks at her watch. Half past eight. Once again a surge of anger courses through her. Who the hell does he think he is? Skipping out the door like that, as if he couldn't wait to get rid of the ball-and-chain and enjoy himself on his own. Which means eyeing up the local talent, of course. As if she didn't know him well enough to guess what his motives are. Suddenly she feels lonely. In a foreign city, on her own. Okay, maybe not on her own – but she might as well be. Anger buoys her up again. Well, she's damned if she's going to sit around waiting for him. At least, not this time. Better take her mind off things. And show him that he can't take her for granted.

~

She gets out of the lift and walks through the foyer of the hotel. A quick shower and a change of clothes has helped her morale. Leave the key at reception. That way Carl can't complain if he has to wait – and she is going to make him wait.

"*Buona sera, signora*," says the man at the reception desk.

"*Buona sera*," replies Helen falteringly. "Um –" Rapidly she decides to switch to English; her few phrases of Italian have a way of evaporating precisely when they are needed most. "I wonder if I could leave the key of our room for my – for Mr. Clynch? If you'd tell him that I just went out for a look around?"

"Of course."

"Thank-you."

"*Prego, signora*. Enjoy the evening – it's a very special one here in Pisa."

"Really?"

"Yes – it's the feast of *San Ranieri*, the patron saint of Pisa."

"Well, we timed our visit nicely, didn't we?"

"All the *lungarni* – the quays – are lit up." The man makes sweeping gestures with his arms and nods enthusiastically. "The whole city turns out to see the *luminara*."

Helen smiles briefly and places the key on the desk.

Just her luck. The one time they choose to come over to Pisa, there's some kitsch village fair going on. The whole place lit up. Ghastly neon lights, no doubt. Candy floss. Hurdy-gurdies… And how it irks her that she wasn't able to say straight out, 'leave the key for my partner'. That's what he is, isn't he?

Actually, she is shocked rigid by the irresistible impulse that swamped her to say 'my husband'. Well, that he certainly is not.

Outside on the street there is a festive atmosphere. Traffic must have been cordoned off, because the whole street has filled up with couples, families, and gangs of adolescents. She groans; what is she thinking of, making her way out into this mêlée, to have to battle against this parading flood of noisy, smug humanity? But she can't let him come back to the hotel and find her sitting waiting for him. She knows the way of it: he carefully avoiding any eye-contact as her eyes stalk his, like tintacks waiting to pin down any tell-tale gesture or word, only to be blunted against the vast wall of mute stubborn resistance he puts up against her.

She starts to push her way through the crowds, keeping her handbag clutched tightly to her chest. That's the story of their relationship all right: her predictably waiting for him.

And how long has she been waiting now? She stumbles and then turns around to glare at the idiot who has banged into her heel with his canal-barge shoes. Seven years. She is thirty-four years old and no wiser than when they started going out as to what this relationship means to him.

And what does it mean to her?

She has to get away from this bedlam. A narrow street to her left looks quiet, so she lets a gesticulating group of teenagers file past, and then turns quickly off the main street. Old buildings with austere facades loom up on either side of her, leaving only a ribbon of darkening sky visible above. She wonders whether anybody lives in them; maybe they are public offices. Most of the large high windows are blank, and many others are shuttered. But then, the brass doorbells and name plates are lovingly polished. She walks on further, the click of her heels echoing loudly on the flag-stoned street, the warm air opening up in little eddying currents of velvet around her bare arms and legs. A large arched gateway appears on her right, with long black wrought-iron bars; she walks over and grips their rusty surface. Inside, shadows have turned the white vaulting of a passage way a dull grey, and her eye skims through it, drawn to the dimly lit point at its end. There, the crepuscular light is an opalescent presence hovering over the midsummer splendour of a courtyard garden.

The silence is broken by the snap of a front door lock just beside her: suddenly the air is filled with laughter and voices talking loudly in Italian. Helen draws back from the arch with a feeling of embarrassment, as if she has been caught spying. Three couples spill out onto the street, but they don't appear to notice her and she follows slowly in their wake as they set off down the street. She can't help but notice how happy they all seem: how appreciative the men seem of their partners, how naturally the couples seem to belong together.

The end of the street opens out into a little piazza. In the farthest corner there is a very old church. What to do – trail the happy couples or check out the church?

But does she really want to visit a church? Hardly riveting material for the envious hordes back home – Oh, yes, we had such a great time – I'd really recommend it – the churches just blew me away… Probably closed, though – which would solve the problem.

The main entrance comes more clearly into view, showing that it is still open. The sign on the left reads: *S. Sisto, consacrata nel 1133*. Romanesque, then. Somehow, she could not have faced Baroque splendour. And what are those Islamic-looking ceramic motifs on the façade? Turn to the left and in through the swing door; there is a dull thud as it falls back into place.

❧

The outside world melts away with uncanny ease as a weightless silence carries her inwards. How do churches contrive to have this quality? She can't remember the last time she willingly set foot in one, but something in her is wrenched as she looks around at the strong simple beauty of this empty church. The stillness is palpable. What prayers have these stone columns absorbed, how much supplication, how much praise?

If she were to say a prayer, which way would it go – supplication or praise?

No contest. Dear God, what is she doing with her life? What is this entity that she calls *her* life? There has been some terrible parting of the ways. There used to be the person Helen: nice, easy-going Helen, always trying her best, filled with good intentions, looking out for others. And then this alien entity called her life started inching out from under the murk of some stone; what shifted the stone? For it isn't *her* life at all, it is something bubbling and surging with the shadowy viral force of smoke: unbiddable, unknowable.

What is this life doing to her? Who is it making her turn into? How can this person filled with such corrosive anger be Helen?

Her relationship with Carl is like a high-wire act, where the only balancing pole he has given her is weighted with insecurity and jealousy. She knows this. And the more she seethes in anger at it, the more he keeps her at arm's length. His fear of commitment has created precisely the situation that justifies his fear of commitment in the first place.

What can she do?

Candles gutter in front of the altar, bright and fragile; not since her schooldays has she lit one, but it is a gesture that she suddenly needs to make. Something both outside and above herself. She is weary with the whole situation, and increasingly frightened; she's thirty-four years old, for god's sake! There isn't very much room for manoeuvre left. The best years of her life have probably gone – and for what?

As she inserts the lighted candle into the narrow holder, the cries of the swifts outside in the piazza break through the barrier of silence. The urgency in their shrillness is unsettling. Her eyes run the length of the nave, then rise to the rose window, as the hairs on her arm, like sea-anemones brushed by water, avert the faintest touch of air.

Time to go.

Once outside in the gathering darkness, she can see a large piazza farther ahead. Handsome, spacious, it is being traversed by groups of people who all seem to be heading in the same direction. She pauses to look up at the sky – it gets dark here much earlier than at home – noticing that the clouds are still quite threatening. Then the floodlighting comes on, throwing the facades of the wide circle of buildings into stark relief. Why not follow the crowd for the moment – they, surely, know where they are going.

Out into what looks like a medieval street, very narrow and overhung with jutting balconies. Less jostling and pushing than she feared – the crowd is good-humoured and high spirits crackle through the air. She begins to relax.

"*Bella*," says a male voice softly behind her left ear.

Her swivelling head encounters a pair of very dark eyes at the same level as her own. A wide smile reveals white teeth, and crinkles the skin at the corners of the dark eyes. Flustered, she turns away.

"*Americana?*" comes the voice again. She doesn't reply. "*Inglese?*" it insists. She feels a hand on her bare shoulder. Her head whips around and she glares at him. He raises his arms in mock alarm. "Sorry," he grins, switching to English, "you not be offended, okay?"

Blue denim shirt, about twenty eight, disarming smile. She turns away again, the sense of panic subsiding.

"You know *San Ranieri*, you seen this before?" The voice is half pleading, half jocose. "This something special, you know?" She glances at him. "I show you – yes? – I show you, please." She frowns. "No," he shrugs expressively, "You not be angry." Another smile, half charm, half shyness. "This very special; I show you." She looks at him for a long moment, relishing the admiration she sees in his eyes, and softening at their trepidation.

"Come," he says, taking her under the elbow.

Now is the moment to tell him to get lost. But her mouth won't open, and she can't bring herself to wrench her arm from his grasp. She feels all the rigidity of a mechanical doll on run-down batteries; only the forward surge of the crowd keeps her moving. All the while she is keenly aware of his hand on her arm and her inability to say anything.

Up ahead the crowd seems to be dispersing into a larger space. The hand on her arm turns her round.

"Now we getting near to *Lungarni*. Is better you not look until we get there. Bigger surprise this way." He takes her other hand in his. "I cover your eyes, or you walk backward – which you prefer?"

"Neither, actually."

Deftly, he begins to steer her backwards through the crowd. "Only a little more. Then you see why." Suddenly he stops. "Now look." Slowly he turns her around.

Gold light coruscating against the shadowy night sky bursts upon her. Like shimmering flame-coloured threads embroidering black velvet, a myriad of dancing guttering candles outlines all the darkened windows of the tall *palazzi* lining the quays.

"But it's real!" breathes Helen. She smiles delightedly.

Her companion laughs and pulls her into the throng.

She lets herself be pulled along; her sense of defiance gets the upper hand over any anxiety she feels. The guy fends a way through the crowd, throwing a look back over his shoulder now and again to make sure she's okay, pointing out the landmarks, grinning at the small children eating wads of candyfloss bigger than their faces, smiling shyly at her.

As they approach another bridge, he stops at a stall and buys what look like two sandwiches.

"*Schiacciata*," he says, holding out one of them to her. "It's good. Taste. Tomato, mozzarella, basil." This he pronounces 'bayzeel'.

Helen takes hers and he leads them to the wall overhanging the river. He gives her a hand up, and then gets up too. They eat their *schiacciata* in silence. All around them the surge of movement and noise from the crowd, the flickering light of the candles, and higher up still the dark recesses of the sky.

He jumps down from the wall. "Come," he says, beckoning her, "I show you other nice thing here in Pisa." He indicates the far side of the river.

She stays where she is on the wall. But it's too early to go back to the hotel. If Carl said he'd be back in an hour, she can safely make it two. She jumps down.

Half on edge, half curious, she begins to cross the bridge. They stop in the middle and he points out the graceful curve of the buildings as they follow the bend in the wide river. In the far distance she can make out the blacker mass of some mountains. Then he directs her attention to the other side, and a white building.

He takes her hand again and they draw up to it. "Pretty church, no?"

"Yes." A Gothic construction of minute proportions, with an abundance of finely wrought white stone – turrets, spires, decorations – make it seem dainty rather than imposing.

"This the oldest part of Pisa," he says, pointing to the narrow alleyways that lead off the main road at regular intervals. Abruptly he turns to her and says, "You very beautiful." Inexplicably his face grows sad, and he looks away.

Helen is nonplussed. Best to shrug the comment and his reaction off. Italians are notoriously melodramatic in these things.

But a part of her is gratified. The part that asks only to be cherished by somebody. And somebody it is; it certainly isn't Carl. She turns to see the guy shaking his head and smiling. He claps his hands together, and says, "Beautiful night, beautiful lady. We go get a coffee, okay?" He gestures towards one of the alleyways. "Get coffee down there."

He takes her hand again and draws her over to the other side of the street. As her feet connect with the uneven flagged surface of the dark alleyway, she has the disconcerting sensation of being outside her body and observing her mute progress.

He stops under a fall of Jasmine from a high wall. "What is your name?"

"Helen."

"Beautiful name!" He laughs softly in the echoing silence.

He draws her on. They turn left, and then right. Or is it left again? She can feel her heart pounding.

And then there it is. A café. She laughs too.

He looks at her shyly. Then cups her face in his hand and kisses her.

Stumbling, she takes a step backwards. His hand falls back down by his side. He says nothing.

"What is your name?" she asks him.

"Abdullah."

She freezes.

The background rumble spills into the bowl of silence holding them. From nowhere, two stray cats shoot mewling and spitting across the alleyway. She starts and a small scream escapes her. Her extremities twitch into life and suddenly she is running, pounding forward, flailing along the darkened alleyway. She hears his voice calling her name, once, twice, and a long third cry. Over the lumpy flag-stones she stumbles, swerving at this corner, then that, no more voice calling, past high graffiti-filled walls, shadowy entrances, until suddenly she re-emerges back onto the quays.

The safety of the milling mass of people. She plunges in. Her breath comes in ragged shuddering gasps.

She is shaking and covered in sweat. And has fallen from grace again. Back to the irritation of shuffling along with the rest.

There is a loud bang from the sky. The crowd surges forward. She exclaims in anger as she is pushed from behind. Another loud bang, and then the sky erupts in a shower of red sparks. Then cold blue. Then icy green. The crowd sighs as a mushroom of golden shards comes falling slowly down through the endless night sky. Some pigeons career out from the roofs of buildings, veering over the top of the crowd in a long steadying arc back to their night-time shelters. All eyes are on the fireworks display. Her eyes stare at the ground as she trudges along.

BABELE

It's that strange, static time of year again in Italy: the growing part of the year over, only now does the heat peak. The swifts are heading back to Africa, their shrill cries fading from the morning and evening skies. And in their wake has come the harsh spasmodic grating of noon-time cicadas. The sound reverberates around the hotel room, intensified by the siesta silence in which the world beyond the closed green shutters is suspended. A world where heat and light circle each other, gathering momentum, until the day spirals into a throbbing paroxysm of death-in-life. Outside, the molten glare of the afternoon sun spills down against the shutters, blistering the paint. Inside, dust motes hover in the muted brilliance.

A bed with an ornate wrought-iron headboard stands against the wall. It is covered with a white cotton bedspread whose cool freshness is impossible to resist in the early afternoon: the only thing to do is pull it back, lie down on the lavender-scented crisp linen sheets, and let the heat wash over me in sleep-inducing waves.

From five o'clock onwards, the heat loosens its grip. A rustling breath of air insinuates itself among the drooping leaves; shutters are opened and curtains on casement windows begin to billow.

I've never managed to rid myself of the idea that there is something decadent about sleeping in the afternoon. At home it would be a nonsense, but here in Tuscany the summer imposes different rhythms. The heat plays havoc with my sluggish blood pressure, draining me of what little energy I have. So the siesta, or *pisolino pomeridiano*, is something I have found I just cannot do without.

My glasses are on the bedside table and I reach out an exploratory hand; the thin metal of the frames meets my fingers. I place the glasses on my nose and things come back into focus. My emaciated legs stretch out in front of me in the bed, poking up through the white linen sheet like two knobbly sticks. The sheet seems more of a shroud than anything else. So I turn it back and slide my legs out onto the blessedly cool terracotta floor. A sip of water from the tumbler on the bedside table, and then I reach for the real stick.

That walking stick is another thing I can't get used to – even though I can't get around without it. It makes me feel doddery. I suppose, however, that that is exactly what I am. How things change. How things decline.

Gingerly I heave myself up into a standing position and make my way over to the window. I undo the catch of the shutters and push them outwards, blinking at the brightness that bursts in on my watery eyes. A breath of air stirs and I raise my face gratefully to it. My room is situated on the first floor, the *piano nobile*, of a *casa torre* that dates back to the *Duecento*. Admirably old, yes, but even then Pisa's Golden Age was over: a brief moment of real splendour that was paid for by an inglorious and lengthy decline. I could choose to go to other more flamboyant cities in Tuscany, but I've been coming here for twenty odd years now and long ago concluded that its vicissitudes strike a peculiar chord with me. Pisa and I companionably share the satisfaction of remembered greatness and the burden of present decay.

Church bells peal out into the late afternoon air. I locate the steeple of Santo Stefano and listen for a moment, reflecting that it must be the six o'clock Angelus. But could it be that late? My watch confirms that it is – I've overslept. Well, it's been a particularly hot day.

The bells ring out their arcane message, evoking pleasing rituals from a distant past in the midst of an even more distant present. I've given up trying to understand what happens in the world – it's all a tasteless mess. My world revolves around art history, it has been my overriding passion for as long as I can remember. A passion, however, that is the source of something close to pain at this stage, for it has become increasingly difficult to give myself up to the immutable beauty of my favourite sculptures and paintings as I become more decrepit. There was a time, you see, when it was easier for me to connect with Michaelangelo's *David* than it was with life: its strength, beauty, and heroic purpose were all that life wasn't. Life was but a series of betrayals of these ideals. And why would I want to connect with that?

I draw back from the window and pass by the bed. It's time to get ready for my evening stroll. My eyes fasten on the mirror straight ahead; the tattered rags on a stick peering back out mock my youthful delusions of grandeur. These days I have to be very careful not to adopt a cynical note when discussing the *David*.

∽

By the time I have got changed and out onto the street, it is a quarter to seven. Strictly speaking, I don't need the panama hat I'm wearing – the evening sunlight is pleasant. But I'm fond of this hat and always wear it. I make my careful way up the street leading towards piazza Garibaldi, as the paving stones can be tricky to negotiate, especially when it rains. That is hardly the case this evening, but the abundant presence of dog excrement renders things problematical in any event, and as an added bonus, the evening breeze brings a very disagreeable odour of urine from the side streets. Not the best for working up an appetite, really.

Piazza Garibaldi is thronged with people, above all young people. Young parents proudly wheeling the next generation of proud parents around in expensive prams; elegantly dressed professional men with brief cases; voices ringing out; friends being greeted with a kiss on each cheek; scooters revving up, filling the air with petrol fumes; students. It's easy to spot the students, dressed in the regulation scruffy jeans, t-shirt and rucksack. With three third level institutions in the city, they never disappear, even in July and August. A group of them has gathered around the statue to enjoy enormous cones of ice-cream. The conversation is animated – they're probably philosophising about the state of the country, or the deleterious effects of capitalism. Or the meaning of life. But, to get to the bottom of that, I suspect you have to have lived it.

Now there's a thing to discuss over an ice-cream: the living of life.

If I had an ice-cream, it would ruin my appetite, so I keep going and make for the *Ponte di Mezzo*, the main bridge in Pisa. The warm air shimmers in the golden sunlight, blending hazily with the suffused radiance of the sky to the west. I position myself right in the middle and follow the wide sweeping curve of the quays along which centuries-old buildings stand sentinel – an austere guard of honour for a fleeting presence that will all too soon melt into the sea.

I am jostled by a young lady, so intent on talking into her mobile phone that she doesn't see me. Then her eyes flick over me, and I see myself for a moment as she must see me: an old man held up by a walking stick. I had got in her way. This is irritating – worse, it is ignorant. I rub my arm and straighten my hat; it is not good for my appetite either.

At that moment, another couple stop beside me at the railings and look down into the slow-moving river. They are both middle-aged, overweight, dressed in shorts and sleeveless t-shirts, and sunburnt. The man's shorts are of the tight white variety favoured at Wimbledon in the Seventies, and he has a pair of white socks on under his open-toed sandals. They speak in English.

"All I want is a decent meal," the man grumbles, "Something that doesn't stink you out with garlic."

"That car- car- carwhatsit we had last night," says his wife, "It didn't have any garlic. But it was still revolting. I mean, when you think of it – raw meat, swimming in oil, with weeds on it!"

I observe them as they move off, and wish them joy in their search for a garlic-less restaurant. They are, of course, in the wrong country. Sometimes I wonder whether mass tourism isn't just another expensive way people have found to be discontented. The internationalisation of provincialism. But that's neither here nor there – above all it's none of my business. I'm beginning to feel gratifyingly peckish; it's time to return to the *Torre di Babele* for the pre-dinner aperitifs.

∾

"*Buona sera, professore!*"

"*Buona sera, Mario.*" I greet the head waiter affably. He's been here since I started coming. We have grown old together, and yet I don't really know anything about him except that his service is always impeccable. But this hotel, the incongruously named *Torre di Babele*, is the closest I have wanted to come to having a home. I return to it for the comfort of an unfamiliar routine, and the absence of – the absence of what? Well, think of the familiar imponderables of a home: the soured relationships; the oppressiveness; the silent rancours; the strangled hopes.

I think I can say that I'm fond of Mario. Nevertheless, without indulging myself in any undue optimism, I'd like to think that my life is equally opaque for him. But there's bound to have been talk – it's the price you pay for returning to the same place year after year. By some mysterious process of osmosis, Mario will have absorbed the fact that I am one of the privileged few who can live on the substantial proceeds of an indulgent aunt's will. *Il professore vive di rendita, sa?* It's not that I have a problem with them knowing this; it's not a crime, after all, is it? Nor do I object to them knowing that my interest in art history is at this stage purely amateurish. Even though I retired long ago from the faction-fighting of academia, my contribution to the body of work on Giovanni Pisano continues to have its admirers.

It's just that my sole wish is to be left in peace. I appreciate all the polite discretion I come in contact with: it's not something you can take for granted. You see, the less contact you have with people, the less chance there is that unpleasantness will seep into your life.

I have a real fear of unpleasantness.

"*Il solito, professore?*" Mario calls out from behind the bar.

I nod, and he takes out the usual bottle of first-rate *prosecco*. The comfort of an unfamiliar routine, as I said. You can't get that *prosecco* back home.

The dining area is much fuller than last night. Of course, it's Saturday evening, and high season at that. I move across to my usual table-for-one by an open window and take my seat as Mario places my glass of *prosecco* in front of me; it is beautifully chilled. A promising selection of canapés then materialises; my mood improves.

"Well! Even for an Italian man, that was just a bit too naughty for my liking!"

"Yeah, right. Pity I didn't see it happening though – I'd've given him what for."

The sound of English cuts through the snatches of French, German and Spanish I have desultorily been listening to. I look up: a party of four has just come into the dining-room, a man and three women. My eyes focus on the woman and man who have just spoken. "I wouldn't mind giving him what for myself," says the woman in the Cockney tones that have overrun England. She laughs loudly and pokes the man in the ribs.

"Uh – right…" The man smiles nervously and then throws a conciliatory glance at one of the other women in the group. "Uh – excuse me," he catches Mario's eye, "Could we have a table for four?" His accent is American.

Mario shows them to a table very near my own and gives them their menus. They scan them in silence.

"Well!" says the Englishwoman, "I don't know about you lot, but first things first. What are we having to drink?"

"Ah, fair play to you, Pauline," cuts in the third woman, "you have your priorities right anyway." Her accent is Irish. "White or red?"

"What do you mean, Nora? Surely that should be white *and* red?"

The women called Nora and Pauline laugh at length, while the other woman glances uneasily at the man.

"Um –" She pauses and Pauline and Nora look up from their menus. She clears her throat and continues, nodding slowly as she speaks. "Um, I think I'll just stick with mineral water." She smiles demurely. "But you go right ahead and have whatever you want. Don't pay any attention to little old me!"

"You sure, Cassie?" enquires the man.

"Absolutely, Jeff."

Now here's an interesting scenario: three different nationalities gathered for a meal, maybe even on holiday together. In reluctant fascination, I place my nearly-empty glass back down on the table.

Pauline is the first to show signs of uncharitable impatience. "Yes, well, whatever," she raps out, one eyebrow arching. "Each to his own, I always say. Shall we get on with it then, and order?"

"I'm with you on that one," says Nora, "I could be doing with a glass of wine after all that tramping around museums in the heat. Tiring, wasn't it?" She looks around at the others.

"Definitely," replies Pauline. "I'm whacked. There's only so much culture a body can take in a day. Even if it was the – what was the name of the museum again?"

"The Uffizi," Cassie promptly informs her. "And I find that in the heat, the best thing for thirst is water."

Nora's eyes glaze over; she nods silently and looks away. Pauline's eyebrows practically disappear into her hairline. "Thanks for the pearl of wisdom dear," she says, "No doubt it will be of some use after we've got through the wine."

I try to concentrate on the canapés in front of me. I'm not at all sure I want to have to listen to this for the rest of the evening. As I select one, Jeff's voice intrudes.

"I wonder what the tour guide has lined up for us tomorrow?" he asks. "Will it be more museums?" His expression is less than enthusiastic. "I wouldn't mind crashing out on a beach somewhere."

"No." The other three stop to look at Cassie; she had uttered the monosyllable with a certain forcefulness. "No," she continues, shaking her head slowly, "I don't think that would be a good idea."

"Why not, honey?" Jeff enquires mildly.

"I read about the beaches here. There are topless women all over the place, and I wouldn't feel at all comfortable with that. European women may feel okay about it – they're a lot more free and easy with their bodies than we are – but where I come from, it's just not the done thing. Actually, it's quite shocking. Right, Jeff?"

"Uh – right, honey," confirms Jeff, with more regret than conviction.

"To say nothing about the *men* on the beaches!" Pauline laughs, a rumbling wheeze suggesting a long-standing attachment to the gin bottle and industrial quantities of cigarettes. "Oooh, but they are naughty!" she takes up. "Too dark for my liking though. I mean, you find yourself wondering just how clean they really are… Everything in this part of the world seems to be either dirty or corrupt."

"Or even both," says Nora.

"But so wonderfully exotic!" says Jeff.

"That's true," says Cassie. "Three weeks of it, though, is more than enough. I'll be glad to get back to civilization."

"Oh, me too dear!" says Pauline. "I'll be glad to get back to a place where you can take efficient service for granted. I mean – they're just so lazy here." She looks over towards the bar and, failing to catch Mario's eye, clicks her fingers loudly until he nods and begins to head towards their table. "Right, then," she says, "everyone ready to get their order in?"

Mario stops at my table as well and takes my order. "*Sono delle parti sue, quelli lì, no?*" His question has the tone of a confirmation: these individuals must all be my compatriots. In one fell swoop he has eliminated national boundaries and racial differences and come up with an anglophone über-state that is decidedly unappealing. I feel put out, but before I have time to reply, he continues with an expressive grimace, "*Dio bono – tre bottiglie hanno preso.*" He's shocked at the number of bottles of wine they have ordered. Then he adds, "*Ci date dentro con l'alcool voi altri stranieri, eh professore?*" The gist, of course, is that all foreigners are a collection of boozers.

He moves off and I look down at my staid little glass of *prosecco*. I have never known him to be so outspoken and am more than a little irritated that I had to be on the receiving end of it. It's not as if I have spent the last twenty years single-handedly depleting the hotel's wine cellars. Neither have I spent them clicking my fingers at him. I glance over at the next table and feel a surge of dislike. Why did they have to come and disturb the agreeable equilibrium we had here? Why can't they rise above the pettiness that leads to these deplorable reactions? Why not try instead to move beyond the predictable confines of their prejudice? I find myself wishing that I didn't understand English – I wouldn't have had to hear all that nonsense. So much for me doing my bit to contribute to the jollification of nations. My hand hovers over the last canapé, but I push it away.

Then once again the conversation at the next table obtrudes upon my attention.

"We're pretty well surrounded in England," says Pauline, pulling tetchily on a cigarette. "I mean, look at the Irish – they're a lot darker than us as well. That's what makes us so different."

Nora looks fazed. Here, evidently, is something she feels it incumbent upon herself to agree with – at least in theory. But the facts are, unfortunately, against her.

Puzzled, Jeff looks from one to the other. "But," he says, "you have the same colouring …"

"Right," agrees Cassie. "And anyway, you're pretty much the same in most other ways too. No big differences that we can see." The Americans look at each other and shrug.

It is hard to say whether Pauline or Nora is more horrified at this unexpected turn of events.

"But – but – " splutters Pauline.

"God almighty!" expostulates Nora. "There are differences between us that you can't even begin to understand. Differences that go back hundreds of years. For instance – "

She is cut short by Jeff, who says, "So let's not even try, okay? We're not that bothered anyway."

A tense silence falls.

Then a man enters the dining-room. He is Italian, very dark, and well-dressed in a showy sort of way. His eyes dart around the room until they come to rest on Pauline. He smiles slightly and heads towards her. She has stopped talking and is looking at him mesmerised as he approaches the table.

"I need talk with you," he says. "Alone." He extends a hand.

"So naughty …" she murmurs, taking the hand and immediately getting to her feet.

He whispers something to her as they disappear out the door together, and her burst of laughter once again fills the dining-room.

"Persistent, isn't he?" says Nora. Her eye lingers on the empty door.

Mario arrives over with the dinner plates and begins to place them in front of the English-speaking contingent. He pauses at the empty seat. I know that he has seen Pauline disappear out the door in the company of that man. "Back in keetchen?" he asks, pointing to the extra dinner.

"Sorry?" Uncomprehending shrugs greet Mario's attempt at English. He scratches his forehead. Then he turns to me. "*Professore, per cortesia,*" An expressive shrug. "Trraanslate!" He glances at the group and shakes his head. "*Che io 'un ce la fo' con quest' inglese.*"

I do not doubt that Mario feels no inclination to get to grips with English; it falls to me to act as linguistic intermediary.

"So," says Cassie, nodding slowly all the while, "you speak English."

"I do," I reply.

"And isn't it just as well you're fluent at the old Italian too!" adds Nora. "Why don't you join us?"

Offhand, I can think of at least a dozen good reasons for not joining them, frankly. But one cannot overly indulge these reactions. I smile politely and begin to shake my head. "Thank you, but – "

"Ah , go on!" says Nora, "you might as well."

"Yeah – come over and join us!" adds Jeff expansively. Cassie nods in agreement.

I have no choice but to give in; anything else would be ungracious.

It proves to be an infelicitous move. Conversation, such as it is, is predictably tedious.

"Are you here on holiday too?" enquires Jeff.

"In a manner of speaking."

"Are you enjoying it?" asks Cassie.

"Immensely."

"Yes, it's a very beautiful country," says Nora. "Even the weather is great. It makes such a change from the drizzle and fog back home."

"I'm sure."

"You know, I'd live here just for the weather," continues Nora, "it must be great to be able to count on sunshine."

"Indeed. That's why I live here for most of the year."

"You live here for most of the year?" echoes Nora, taken aback.

So far, so innocuous. But I can feel it coming. The sniping will start.

"Yes," I reply, and then add for good measure, "It must be at least twenty years now."

"Gee!" exclaims Cassie.

"Well how about that!" says Jeff.

"Although, I don't know …" Nora sits back from the table and folds her arms. Here we go, I think. "I couldn't *live* here," she informs me, "not even for a certain period of the year. It's grand for a once-off holiday, but that's it." She takes a sip of her wine, and continues, warming to her theme. "Do you not find that it's too dirty, and too corrupt?" Without waiting for an answer, she ploughs on. "All the buildings are so unkempt. And there's nothing special about Pisa. I mean, why would you choose to stay in such a backwater?"

"I could ask the same thing of any Irish person who chooses to stay on in Ireland." I smile perfunctorily.

Jeff guffaws. Cassie titters. Nora is not amused.

"All the violence here, as well." Nora taps the table with her finger. "It's a disgrace. I know somebody who was mugged at gun-point here last summer."

"Shocking," I concur, "and they're not even keeping up with the latest developments. Dublin, I believe, is in the vanguard there. Muggings at syringe-point, if I'm not wrong?"

Nora blinks rapidly, and then sniffs. "I wouldn't know – it's never happened to me."

We survey each other with mutual hostility until Nora looks away. My patience is wearing very thin. I should have known better and avoided all contact: their kind of provincialism has always been abhorrent to me.

Nora takes another sip of her wine and then turns back to Jeff and Cassie. "I wonder if that's the last we'll see of Pauline this evening?"

"Who knows," replies Cassie. "She's something else though, isn't she Jeff?"

"Uh – right, yeah, she's something else."

"Picking up a man like that, and going off with him. That takes some nerve."

"Or just bloody good luck," mutters Nora.

"All I know is that I couldn't," Cassie states flatly. "I'd heard things were different in Europe." She smiles her demure smile. "Pauline seems to have those free and easy European ways, all right."

"No – just plebeian ways."

There is an audible intake of breath. Oh dear, I think, now how did that slip out? I confess that I'm shocked – almost as shocked as those sitting around me. In effect, it's not the type of thing one likes to hear anyone coming out with, still less oneself. So tasteless.

I look around at the raised eyebrows and the lowered eyes.

FALLING STARS

The water splashed over the blue and white ceramic plate, taking the remains of the starter with it. She placed it in the marble sink on top of the other three plates. A burst of laughter came in from the veranda through the open kitchen door, and she smiled to herself. It was half past nine on an August evening, and the sky was all but dark: to the west, a faint glimmer of yellow, topped by a virulent streak of green, was all that remained of a vivid sunset.

She wiped her hands on a tea-towel, and then opened the oven. The fish was cooked, so she removed the four portions wrapped in tin foil and distributed them on the plates. Then she turned to the mixed salad and gave it a final toss.

"You need help, Rosemary?"

She jumped at the voice breaking in on her thoughts, and then shook her head at such silliness. "It's all right, Valeria," she replied, turning to look at the woman framed by the kitchen door. "I'll manage," she added, smiling.

"As you prefer…" Valeria shrugged and headed back out to the veranda.

Rosemary looked after her anxiously, afraid that she might have taken offence in some way. Or maybe Valeria was just bored by the company. Anyway, it wouldn't do to get too worked up about it. Finding an old farmhouse for them to come and stay in must have taken up a lot of her time, and yet she'd been so obliging about the whole thing. Brian and herself had been delighted at the prospect of staying for a week in the Tuscan countryside, and so they'd given Valeria the go-ahead to act as mediator and rent the farmhouse on their behalf. The owners, an elderly couple by the name of Cecconi, had evidently come into some money. They had promptly abandoned the rigours of their peasant existence in the *casale* in favour of a modern detached *villetta* in the nearby town of San Miniato, from where – and not without a certain hilarity – they pocketed the proceeds accruing from tourists who wished to get back to nature.

The first sighting of the farmhouse had not disappointed Rosemary or Brian As they wound up the narrow dusty road in the car in the late afternoon sunshine, it had materialized from behind its enclosed isolation of olive trees. In a natural hollow half way up the hill, its two storeys squatted solidly, protected from the wind by a couple of colossal cypress trees placed at either end. It hadn't been plastered over, and the large roughly hewn red bricks gave off a subdued glow in the slanting golden light. Green shutters framed the smallish windows, from which hung scarlet trailing geraniums. There were no balconies. But Rosemary's heart had swelled when she saw the spacious rectangular veranda that was attached to the kitchen at the farthest end of the house. She had stood in front of it and linked her arm through Brian's, picturing the breakfasts and dinners that they could have within its sturdy columns.

Naturally they had wanted to invite Paolo and his wife Valeria to dinner there. Brian and Paolo went back a good while – seventeen years at this stage! She and Brian had already been going out when they first met Paolo, who had come over to her husband's department to do some research on international company law and get a qualification in English. How things had changed since then. Brian had progressed to Senior Lecturer and Paolo was a *Professore Ordinario*. He had also married Valeria. Rosemary scrunched up the greasy bits of tin foil and threw them into the bin. She didn't know Valeria very well, really, and it was proving difficult to get any kind of decent conversation out of her that evening. She sighed. Well, the next course was ready anyway.

"Brian," called Rosemary, "could you bring out the salad bowl and the bread?" There was no point in disturbing their guests. But no reply came from outside. Rosemary listened, poised with two dinner plates in her hands. No, conversation was continuing unabated. "Brian!" she called again. The low rumble of the men's voices halted.

"What?" asked Brian, his brevity betraying just the slightest hint of irritation.

"Nothing," replied Rosemary, throwing her eyes to heaven. "I'll take care of it myself." She brought the plates out to Valeria and Paolo. And then, after two further trips to the kitchen, they could all begin to eat.

Rosemary surveyed the table to check that everyone had what they needed. She glanced around the veranda as well: yes, the citronella candles were a real addition. They flickered in the warm dark air, sending shadows scurrying up the walls and creeping over the pavement. Hopefully they'd also keep some of the plague of mosquitoes at bay.

"So that's why old Barton was the laughing stock of the department," Brian said, slicing into the fish on his plate. Rosemary looked at him blankly, but then Paolo gave his peculiarly noiseless laugh, punctuated by little popping breaths.

"He seemed so – how can I say – so meticulous when I first met him," he commented. The mirth suddenly faded from his face. "But when you don't research your sources properly, this sort of thing is bound to happen." He too took a measured forkful of the fish.

Rosemary hoped that they liked it. It was always a bit nerve-wracking having to cook for Italians. She glanced from Brian to Paolo.

"Anyway," took up Brian, "he's well past his prime. He's got a bit decrepit as of late, and that can't be good for the Department."

Rosemary looked down at her plate.

"It's good," said Valeria.

Rosemary looked back up. "Oh, thanks Valeria – I'm glad you like it."

"Yes, it's great," said Brian, "very nice indeed. Like some more wine, Paolo?

"No, thank you – I've had enough," replied Paolo. "And yes, the fish is good, Rosemary. It's some consolation; you didn't make any pasta." He smiled briefly at her.

"Oh, please!" cut in Valeria, with a brusqueness that startled Rosemary, "Don't tell me that you can't survive without your dish of pasta for one evening?" She regarded him, one eyebrow arched. *Ci dobbiamo sempre far conoscere, noialtri italiani, eh?*"

"My wife says that we Italians always make a show of ourselves," said Paolo. Carefully, he placed his fork on the dinner plate. "I hope," he added, glancing briefly at Valeria, "you won't be demonstrating that this evening."

Valeria's hand, which had been pulling on a lock of hair, froze. She turned to Brian. "I'd like some more wine."

"White or red?" asked Brian.

"White."

As Brian leaned across the table to fill her glass, Paolo stared at her. "That's the third glass you've had," he said coldly.

"You've bothered to keep a count…" Valeria sat back into her chair and raised her glass in a mock toast to her husband. "Well, now at least I know how to get your attention." She took a mouthful.

Paolo sat back into his chair and folded his arms.

Rosemary glanced quickly at Brian. "Here," she said, "fill me up while you're at it. It was thirsty work in there."

Brian complied without a word. Rosemary took a sip of her wine, trying desperately to think of something to say to dissipate the charged silence.

"And how are your children?" Valeria's voice broke the tension. "You have two, don't you?"

"Yes, that's right," answered Rosemary quickly, "a boy and a girl." She took another sip of her wine. "Oh – um, and yes – they're fine, great …" She smiled in confusion.

"Where are they staying?"

"They're with their grandparents – my parents."

"Are they like you or Brian?"

"Well, I suppose – "

Paolo interrupted. "Why do you always have to ask such personal questions?" He shook his head and turned to Rosemary. "How is your teaching going?"

"Great." she replied.

"Excellent, excellent." Paolo paused for a moment before adding, "Tell me about the programme – no, the syllabus – that you are doing at the moment." He turned expectant eyes on her.

Rosemary glanced at Brian, but he was concentrating on cutting a slice of bread and refilling his own glass. She couldn't account for it, but she was beginning to feel on edge. "Um, next year I'll be concentrating on the Victorian novel and Romantic poetry."

"Oh, how very interesting. But nothing contemporary?"

"Not next year."

"Mmmm. A pity. There's that marvellous poet, who's just published a new collection – what's his name…"

Oh, bloody hell, thought Rosemary, what cutting-edge genius was he going to pull out of the hat now? Should she throw caution to the winds and, irrespective of the name, say yes! wow! she knew him too, and roll off a few gushing adjectives? She looked at him steadily, waiting for the pearl of wisdom.

Then Valeria yawned loudly. Rosemary seized her chance. "Shall we have the pudding, perhaps?" She looked around the table, and without waiting for an answer, got up and went into the kitchen.

She paused for a moment, ran a hand through her hair, and then turned to the sink. The plates had to be washed for the pudding and she got through them rapidly, scrubbing just a little too zealously perhaps. Then she felt a presence behind her. Valeria was at the door holding the dinner plates; she placed them on the draining board. She glanced at Rosemary and said shortly, "I'll bring in the salad and bread. I think we'll leave the wine bottles. Okay?"

"Fine by me," said Rosemary, watching her disappear out the kitchen door.

Pudding was a peach mousse, accompanied by *spumante*, which should have sweetened the atmosphere. Brian scraped his plate with his spoon and said, "That was delicious, I must say." He winked at Rosemary and took a mouthful of his *spumante*. Then it was back to the intricacies of departmental politics. "So, basically Higgins got his funding for the conference, all right. His performance at the faculty meeting was masterful, and the upshot of it was that research funds for the two junior lecturers that year were siphoned off to him for it. Let's just say that he's supplanted old Barton as most-hated-man in the Department."

"Yes," said Paolo, "How do you say – there were no flies on him, right?"

"Right," answered Brian laughing, "Above all when you think that the conference is basically an excuse for him to have the youngest and tastiest of his female students all gathered adoringly in the one space. Like some kind of a harem, with him presiding over things like a bloody Pasha. How to get paid for mixing business with pleasure, eh? Maybe we should all be taking notes from him – the sly dog!"

The two men laughed; one silently, the other uproariously.

Rosemary looked at her forty-five-year-old husband guffawing with relish at the prospect of his own harem, and she suddenly felt an irrepressible need to get away from the table for while. She stood up and glanced over at Valeria, who was pouring herself another glass of wine. Paolo didn't even notice. Brian had launched into some other tale.

"I think I'll just take a turn around the garden," she said quietly.

Valeria nodded.

∽

Away from the house and its lights, there was a surprising luminosity in the clear night sky. It was full of stars, and to her right a pale moon hung against its dark blue recesses. The wind whispered in the trees and shrubs around her. She lowered her head and adjusted her sight to the deep shadows. There were oleander shrubs here and she could get their faint cherry-vanilla scent. Then, from the corner of her eye, she saw something dart past her. She turned to look. There in the bower of trees ahead, a number of fireflies flitted and bobbed in an arcane dance. Entranced, she watched the minute fairy lights as they retreated in further amongst the trees.

She breathed in deeply and looked back up at the sky. And then a shooting star fleeted across it, leaving an evanescent silver froth in its wake. It faded. Rosemary's eyes darted here and there. And another one shot overhead. And then another. Followed by a whole shower of them, fizzling and splintering across the heavens. Silent speed, spectacularly fragile, hardly noticeable unless you took the trouble to look. What wish could she make?

A tear rolled down her cheek; she brushed it away impatiently. She'd go and tell Brian – she wanted him to share this with her.

⁂

"Of course!" cried Valeria. "I'd forgotten. Here we call this *la notte di San Lorenzo*. Saint Laurence's Night. It's the night of the *stelle cadenti.* "

"Ah, the night of the shooting stars," said Rosemary.

"The falling stars," added Valeria, looking away.

"Well, I suppose we'd better go and see," said Brian, rising from his chair to stand beside Rosemary. "Are you two coming?"

Valeria downed the rest of her glass of wine and stood up without a word. Paolo's expression became supercilious. "Go on without me. I don't want to ruin my digestion, running around the garden in the dark."

They waited under the trees but nothing materialized. Rosemary felt a bit of a twit – had she merely imagined the whole thing?

"I'm beginning to get a crick in my neck," complained Brian. "Do you think this is going to take much longer?"

"Hang on while I look in my crystal ball," replied Rosemary, with a touch of sharpness.

Valeria laughed softly. Then she said, "A terrible massacre happened here in San Miniato, on this day you know, back in 1944." She paused to look at them both, and then added, "It was made into a film by the Taviani brothers." Her forefinger and thumb rounded in a gesture of appreciation. "Have you ever seen it?"

Rosemary and Brian shook their heads. "So what happened?" enquired Brian.

"Well, the Americans, they were advancing up through Italy and they had reached Tuscany." Valeria paused again. "The Germans were retreating, taking prisoners with them."

Rosemary nodded. "I can imagine the chaos,"

"Ooff! It was a terrible situation. Actually, the old people say it was different to the film."

Rosemary shifted to her other foot. "Aren't things always..."

"Anyway," continued Valeria, "the Germans, they didn't want to be slowed down by the women and children. So they made them stay with the parish priest, in the safety of the church." She paused and shook her head. "But it was an American bomb that blew the church to bits."

"My God," exclaimed Rosemary.

"Yes – the things people do to each other..."

"Dear oh dear," said Brian, "another nail in the coffin of international relations, what?" He rubbed his hands and, cocking an eyebrow at Rosemary, announced, "Yes – well, I think I've done enough star-gazing for tonight. I wouldn't mind a glass of grappa."

"That sounds great," said Valeria.

Rosemary shrugged.

⌒

Brian poured out a glass of grappa for himself and Valeria, and Rosemary had another glass of the almost-flat *spumante*. Paolo took nothing.

"You've had too much to drink." He watched Valeria as she knocked back the contents of the glass in one go. Brian was looking at her in delight. "Ah, so that's how it's done, is it?" he said, impressed, and promptly knocked his own back. "Have another!" he added expansively, and refilled her glass and then his own.

"You've had enough." Paolo's tone was icy. His eyes darted in Valeria's direction, but slid away again before meeting hers.

Suddenly she banged her glass back down on the table. "Don't tell me what I can or can't do!" she said, her voice rising.

Rosemary glanced at Brian; he looked nonplussed. "Do you want a coffee?" she asked him.

"Um, not just at the moment," he replied.

"Maybe *you* should have a coffee, Valeria," Paolo interjected.

There was a moment of silence. "That's all you've ever done in my life," she said to him slowly, "set yourself up as a judge. You always know best." She shook her head and then turned on him. "You make me sick."

"Well, it's mutual." Paolo folded his arms again and sat right back into his chair.

Rosemary was horrified. She didn't dare bring up the topic of coffee again, even though they could all do with some. Brian was looking more and more fuddled. She shifted uneasily in her chair. What should she do?

A flush now mottled Valeria's neck and throat. "All those decisions that you made for me," she said, looking down at her hands, "all those right decisions..." Suddenly she looked back up at Paolo and her hands had become clenched fists. "You were right about everything."

"There's no need to involve Rosemary and Brian in your paranoia," Paolo said, "Why do you have to say all this in front of them? You're an exhibitionist."

"I want them to know what kind of a man you really are. Why shouldn't they know? Are you worried you'll lose face?" But she didn't wait for an answer and, leaning forward in her chair, she hissed at him, "You've left me with nothing. No husband – you're not a *husband* – no life –" She paused, and then spat out at him, "And no children."

She bit her lip, her chin beginning to tremble. "That was a really good decision. No children because what would you want to bring them into a world like this for, it would be too selfish, and anyway it was a thankless task." She paused. "You are the selfish monster – *you* have never wanted to give –" She stopped, and then said quietly, "You've left me with nothing." She sat there as if frozen to her chair.

Nobody moved. Nobody spoke. The only sound was the clicking of bats as they flew around in the darkness.

Paolo stood up abruptly. "I think it's time to go." He turned to Rosemary. "Thank you for the meal." Then he turned to Brian, who was still looking baffled. "On my wife's behalf, I apologise for her behaviour."

"Another good decision," mumbled Valeria, getting to her feet. Paolo walked out ahead of her, over towards where they had parked their car. "Sorry," she muttered, not looking them in the eye. She too walked slowly over to the car.

The sound of the car retreated down the road. They looked at each other.

"Well, that beats all," said Brian, shaking his head. "A real case of happy families – or should I say, the lack of them. You'd wonder what got into her. I mean, it wasn't a very nice thing to do, humiliating him like that in front of us. I'm glad you'd never spring anything like that on me."

Rosemary looked at him, and smiled.

A HOUSE OF CARDS

The day begins like any other. I place the mocha coffee-pot on the gas, taking care to leave the lid open so that the liquid will be creamier when it gurgles out of the spout. This is the way my husband prefers it. Soon the rich smell of freshly-made coffee insinuates itself into all the corners of the house. Giacomo, my husband, will materialise any moment now.

"Good morning!" he says, coming briskly into the kitchen adjusting his tie. Something in the air is galvanised; I am conscious of moments passing more rapidly and my early morning torpor begins to fall away. In less than five minutes he will be gone for the day.

He stands in front of me and kisses me on the cheek. "You like this shirt, eh?" he asks. But his eyes have already shifted to the battery charger for his mobile; he removes the mobile and then switches it on. His eyes then come to rest on his briefcase lying flat on one of the chairs. "Ah, there it is," he says. He opens it and starts to check the contents.

I examine the shirt. It's difficult to say why he asks for my opinion on these matters; his taste is much surer than mine, and he has always had more flair in putting colours together. To my mind, only an Italian man could think of wearing a pale pink shirt and look so well. The shirt suits his dark colouring and adds a glow to the remains of his summer tan. Despite my best efforts, my own skin has never managed to lose its wintry pallor.

"It's fine," I answer, and smile.

I hand him his small cup of coffee and he stirs it methodically for a few moments. Then he knocks it back in a couple of sips. His spoon collects the unmelted sugar from the bottom of the cup, which he swallows. This is followed by a glass of water at room temperature. Giacomo never has anything solid to eat for breakfast; he doesn't like to head into a morning's work feeling *appesantito*, as he puts it.

I have to have my fix of brioche and coffee. *Caffè lungo*, as it is known here: a nice comforting mug of hot percolated coffee that you can sit and mull over.

I hear my son Michael before I see him. There is a loud yawn from the kitchen door and then he wanders in, pulling a hand through his fair hair. He shuffles to a halt beside Giacomo. "*Ciao babbo*," he says, stifling another yawn.

"Don't you have a lecture at eight o'clock?" Giacomo enquires, casting an irritated eye over Michael's pyjamas. It's a quarter to eight.

Michael, leaning on the kitchen table, yawns again before answering. "Yeah – I do. It's a two-hour lecture, and as a major concession they've joined the two fifteen-minute pauses before the lectures together; the lecture starts at half past eight now."

Giacomo shrugs. "The Arts faculty," he says morosely, and sighs at length. "It was ever the same. That kind of sloppy approach wouldn't have been tolerated in the Engineering faculty, I can tell you." He resumes checking the contents of his briefcase. Giacomo doesn't approve of Michael's choice of faculty: it's an expensive indulgence that gives no guarantees for the future, as well as filling your head with wishful nonsense. It's all just so much pie-in-the-sky.

Michael knows this; he says nothing and looks away. Our eyes meet.

"Morning Mum," He gives his lop-sided smile and then kisses me on the cheek as well. "Any chance of some coffee?"

"It's already on," I indicate the percolator.

I accompany Giacomo to the front door. "See you at dinner-time," he says, as he does every morning. I busy myself straightening his tie and as he's getting into the lift, call after him, "Drive carefully!" As I do every morning, knowing that Giacomo will drive very prudently indeed.

I have my breakfast standing at the counter, and furtively observe Michael slumped over his at the table. He hasn't said anything to me, and I haven't dared to ask – but I know there's something up with him. Something is weighing on him. There's something strange in his eyes.

A pain twists inside me and I have to turn away. Even with my back to him, I can still see his vulnerable blond head bent over the mug of coffee, the long legs spread-eagled under the table. But it would be as difficult to actually stroke that head as it is easy to imagine myself doing so. Who knows what is going through his mind at the moment, what the cause of his suffering is: his life is a mystery to me. A mystery that is the most precious reality of my own life; so precious that from time to time I am paralysed by the fear he will suddenly be taken from me.

I wasn't much older than Michael is now when I had him.

෴

The house is once again mine until the evening meal. I step out onto the *terrazza* and start to sweep up the fallen leaves. Late September, and there is a nip in the early morning air

– a fresh pungency that had been missing since May. The sky is a clear blue from which all traces of heat-haze have disappeared. Change is streaming invisibly through this air.

It's another Tuscan autumn. And yet, it still seems like something I observe rather than live through.

I pick up the broom and shovel and begin to sweep the dead leaves and withered petals into little heaps. There is no wind, and anyway the *terrazza* is a shaded oasis. Except for one small opening, I have managed to train climbing shrubs in such a way as to give seclusion and shelter. Climbing roses, bougainvillea and plumbago cover the pergola overhead, while mature orange and lemon trees in enormous terracotta vases provide a screen along the external railings. High-rise living means that you can always take prying eyes for granted; it's better to exclude them as much as possible.

I left my own country at twenty-one, and have been living in Tuscany for twenty-six years. So I've spent more time here than the country I was born in. Now I am a wife and mother, and the keeper of a home. I created this *terrazza*: the Italians may have their cuisine and their fashion, but we have our gardening. I put it together with love, bit by bit, watching the passing seasons, noting the changes they brought. Then why is it that the memories of the autumns from home have such a vivid sharpness to them?

The word 'we' has a certain hollowness to it.

September has two very different flavours for me now. One a luscious cornucopia on which I seem to have stumbled by accident; this is the September that Michael will remember with vivid sharpness. September in Tuscany is a time of golden sunlight and mellow stillness: of opulent bunches of grapes, opaque green and velvety purple, hanging from laden trellises throughout the countryside; then piled up in fruit bowls on kitchen tables. It is a time of sweet-tasting figs, of mushrooms, and of pumpkins. This I have come to associate with September.

It's very different to that far-off time of berries, of conkers and Michaelmas daisies, of orange, red and yellow leaves, and a touch of frost in the night-time air.

Here, unlike so much of the fruit, the leaves just grow tired; they haven't got the energy to put on a final display of colour, merely fading, imperceptibly, until they drop off the trees, spiralling palely to the ground.

One type of September floats in at the back of my mind with all the unexpected shock of a ghostly presence, while the cyclical solidity of the other has given the disappearing years of my life a comforting rhythm. But it's a rhythm teetering on the brink of decline, like this September morning.

∾

The copper serving-pan gleams on the kitchen wall, caught in the slanting rays of the late afternoon sun. I give it one last buff, and then stand back to admire my handiwork. Now all the copper jugs, pans and bowls stand in burnished glory on the wooden shelves and hang from the walls. Everything is as it should be in the kitchen. I have always liked the kitchen in the late afternoon, when the chores are done and the sunlight is filtered through the semi-shuttered window in restful beams.

On the way to the *ripostiglio* – I can't bring myself to use the inadequate word store-room – I glance in at the dining-room. It too is peaceful and ordered in the afternoon sun. I have to sort out the change of bedclothes; the bedspreads for this season – the *mezza stagione* – are folded away there. They must be taken out and aired, and the ones we will soon finish using, washed and put away to take their place. The *ripostiglio* is windowless, and for that reason I always leave the door slightly ajar. Now I push it fully open and switch on the light.

There on the shelves in front of me, the jars of tomato conserve made ten days ago present a satisfying sight. They will do us throughout the winter. There are also jars of home-made jam – apricot, peach and damson (carefully picked in August); and the fig and walnut comfiture which I made last week. All labelled and dated.

Sometime I'll have to get round to making the apple jelly I remember from my childhood.

I know exactly where the bedspreads are. I make my way among the various boxes and cases, over to the back wall, and unzip one of the plastic wardrobes that I use for storing *la biancheria*; inside my eye falls immediately on the bedspreads and covers in their vacuum-packed plastic wrapping. Despite the vacuum packing, the packages are bulky, and it is difficult to extract them. I bend down slowly, taking care not to strain my back. Four packages at one go seem to be beyond me – the threat of an attack of lumbago stops me. My arms clutch three and I begin to haul them up from the bottom of the wardrobe. I have almost got them out when I lose my balance and fall heavily against the side of the wardrobe, letting the packages drop to the floor. The wardrobe sways dangerously for a moment, and then, as if in slow motion, I see it keel over into the far corner. On its way to the ground, it bangs off a shelf, and in a flurry of white, sheets and sheets of paper swirl to the floor, while notebooks fall repeatedly with a heavy thud.

I close my eyes, and then open them again. No – the chaos is still there. I sigh at length. *Questo pasticcio proprio non ci voleva*. A mess like this is the last thing I needed: it will take ages to clear up. The wardrobe and its contents will have to be put to rights, and then I'll have to sort through all the note-books and paper scattered over the floor.

Setting the wardrobe to rights isn't actually as difficult as I thought it would be, and soon both it and its contents are back to normal. I take heart, and turn gamely to the forest of paper. It's all old stuff from my teaching days, before Giacomo decided that the wife of a wealthy engineer with a reputation to maintain shouldn't be seen grubbing around the private schools of the city.

I liked teaching. It took me out of myself.

First I pick up the sheets of paper – old lessons, photocopies from grammar books, reading passages – and put them back into their folders. Then I turn my attention to the notebooks. They will have to be stacked. And then unexpectedly a photo album slides out from under some text books. My curiosity aroused, I flick it open.

That face, looking out at me from years ago. My legs buckle and I crumple to the floor. Why did I have to come across this? What unhappy chance decreed that this old wound should be re-opened today?

A moment of happiness immortalised, which the myriad of moments in its wake hasn't managed to dim. The end of term ball, shortly before our Finals. That handsome face; the dress suit; the arm wrapped possessively around my shoulder; the far-away look of the eyes.

I had only felt the possessiveness of his encircling arm. It was a joy to me. The radiant face smiling out at me from the shelter of his arm hardly seems like mine. Was that me?

Far worse what greets me in the mirror now: how can *that* be me? The gratuitous cruelty of time. What need is there to humiliate a body so? And where has the confident gladness of that smile gone to?

Why did Matthew leave me? His decision stunned me. Numbed me. The celebrations for our Finals, the joy and satisfaction. And then the pain of his decision to go off travelling around the world on his own. It was too early to settle down, he had said.

All I knew was that it was too soon to abandon me.

Goaded into action, I too left the country and came to Italy. The job teaching English hadn't been hard to come by. Giacomo was one of my students – although, I had never dared to call him such. The ten years separating us and his obvious experience wouldn't have allowed it.

He proposed very quickly – only ten weeks after we met. The security. The comforting attention he dedicated to me. It was irresistible at the time. I accepted him, and was thrown into a whirlwind of festivities.

Complimenti ingegnere, si è scelto una moglie tanto giovane e bella. I was the young wife who reflected my engineer husband's good taste.

Che sposina deliziosa! And all that a beautiful bride should be.

The first wedding anniversary came and went. I couldn't confess to Giacomo that I was having difficulties adapting to my new role as full-time wife, it would have seemed ungrateful somehow. What a strange time it was: I existed in a cocoon of Giacomo's making, his larger-than-life presence acting as a buffer between me and the outside world. Rather than protect, though, the cocoon began to crush me.

Then that telephone call had come. That voice so shockingly at the other end of the line. He'd inveigled my sister into giving him my address and phone number. Passing through Italy. A meeting – he needed to see me. He had to see me.

With an effort, I bring my eyes back to focus on the photograph. I look at those far-away eyes, and wonder: Did he ever really see me?

I met him. Sick at heart beforehand because of Giacomo, and sick at heart afterwards because of Matthew. We met far from prying eyes: the spartan room in his *pensione* is etched in my mind. His distress at my marriage was a torment. I was the only girl he thought of, the girl that he turned to in his dreams. Yet what could he offer me? He wasn't done seeing the world; he didn't know if his travels would ever be done. He just wasn't made for staying in one place.

Let him go, let him go, let him go.

My cocoon was a welcome refuge after that.

⊂∿

This time I close the door of the *ripostiglio* after me. It is once again in order. I feel like I could do with a long hot bath before dinner.

It is soothing to lay the table in the dining-room. I have decided we will eat there and do things in style. The home-help will clean up tomorrow.

The white damask tablecloth looks well; I take out the Limoges china and place the starched napkins in the dish for risotto. We'll be eating pumpkin risotto. Then I take out the crystal glasses. They pick up the cool white light of the silver condiment set and candlesticks. Last of all, I place the centre-piece of freshly picked sprays of blue plumbago between the candlesticks.

Giacomo arrives punctually at a quarter to eight. We have an aperitif together on the *terrazza*; enough light filters out through the dining-room casement window without us having to use the outside lights.

"How was your day?" I ask him.

"So so," Giacomo replies. "Still under pressure to get that job finished. And now the surveyor has started creating problems." He takes a sip of his aperitif, and then asks,

"And how are you?" Before waiting for an answer, he adds, smiling, "You look very well. I like that colour on you."

I smile too.

I turn away to go into the kitchen and add the finishing touches to the dinner, and find Michael standing there. He is observing us. "*Ciao babbo, ciao mamma,*" he says. "What are you poisoning yourselves with?"

"Get him one as well, will you Giacomo?" I say. On my way past, I give Michael's arm a pat. "We'll be sitting down shortly."

The risotto has turned out well, but Giacomo hardly seems to have tasted it. He is annoyed at the way bureaucracy is holding up an important contract. His voice seems to be louder than usual this evening. I glance at Michael and see that he isn't listening either. He has that look in his eyes again. That far-away look.

SUNDAY LUNCH

As soon as I woke up, I realised there was something different. In the dim light of early morning, I shifted in the bed, careful not to disturb Massimo. My husband. How strange those words sounded, and yet what pleasure they gave. I turned to the dark head on the other pillow. It was strange how much those words affected me, I hadn't been prepared for this rush of tenderness; happiness bubbled up from deep inside and I smiled.

The casement window was open ajar and I turned back to it. Then suddenly it came to me. There was an echo in the air.

Through the filtering slats of the closed shutters, the reverberation was unmistakeable. A returning presence after months of heat, it was a familiar shock which our long honeymoon in the Seychelles had almost duped me into forgetting. The echo reached my ears as a dull rumble, as if the cooling air of early November had fragmented into brittle particles that grated against each other. This earth-bound echo would be a leaden presence until warm air once again breathed over the dark earth.

The belligerent piping of a blackbird broke through the still air. I pictured him perched on some nearby aerial overlooking the red tiles of the city roofs, stridently staking his daybreak claim to whatever bit of territory he had marked out for himself. And then from the balcony came the soft cooing of pigeons, and the sudden flap and whir of startled wings. A quick glance at the alarm clock showed it was ten past seven. Well, why not get up and quietly prepare a Sunday breakfast for Massimo – something he really liked. I sat up on my elbow and looked down at his sleeping form. A bare shoulder protruded from the covers and I bent my head to it; his skin smelt of warmth and intimacy. I kissed it.

My slippers padded noiselessly over the floor, out into the hall. Two large suitcases stood against the wall opposite the front door, more or less where they had been left yesterday afternoon. I would have preferred to take a leisurely day to unpack and settle back in, but a family lunch at Massimo's was unavoidable. A sense of discomfort intruded. No, I was not looking forward to the Sunday ritual. There would be the usual mill of relatives that descended on Massimo's family home every second Sunday. Massimo loved these family reunions, and thrived in a room full of the people he loved best in the world, as he said; I have to confess I usually found them an ordeal, coming away as I did with more than a few scratches. Massimo laughed it off, saying that they didn't mean any harm, that was just the way they were. There was no point in being too thin-skinned as there was nothing personal in it. I chewed on my lip. Well, better to get on with it – it mightn't be that bad. Anyway, what else could I do; I was, after all, now a member of the family. Surely it would be enough for them to see that Massimo was happy.

Massimo, Massimo – my brand new, shiny bright husband, who loved me with an intensity that dazed at times; but who was complaining? When this fragile realisation would creep up on me, what a joy it was to let it ease through to those secret corners of my being that hadn't believed they would ever be healed in this way. He was that one special person who had made me glad to be myself and no-one else; and in bringing out the best in me, I gave him back the best of himself. We were meant for each other.

The kitchen was dark so I made my way over to the window and opened it. Then I lifted the catch on the shutters, which squeaked in protest. The shutters themselves were also stiff and it was a strain to push them back into place on the wall. The sun was still hidden by the mountains encircling the city, but it had imbued the sky with a pearly yellow radiance against which the dark indigo mass of the mountains was thrown into sharp relief. Goosebumps broke out on my arms and I shivered, drawing back from the window. Hopefully the condominium would switch the heating on soon.

Thank goodness I'd had the unusual presence of mind to do a small shopping before everything closed yesterday evening; I removed the butter, milk and eggs from the fridge and placed them on the worktop beside the stove. I fetched the *pancarré* from the press and hummed as I got the mocha coffee-pot ready. A fridge that was decently full was certainly a better start to married life than the Old Mother Hubbard syndrome – what was it the Italians said, *il buon giorno si vede dal mattino*? If the weather is good at the start of the day, it'll be good for the rest of the day. Well, it was a proverb that could never be applied in my benighted part of the world, in thrall to every flurry of wind that gusted in off the Atlantic. Or the Steppes, for that matter. Sun before seven, rain before eleven. And, as people said, not without a touch of self-commiserating, perverse pride, you could get the four seasons all in a single day.

I paused, carton of milk in one hand, half-full saucepan in the other. A good start is most of the battle, that was the Italian approach. Or, start as you mean to go on.

There was a movement at the door and I turned around. Massimo was looking at me, head on one side, eyes intent.

"A very good morning to my wife," he said. "You're up early."

"You know how it is when you're happy." I crossed quickly over to him. "And I'm very happy," I added, kissing him.

His arms enfolded me.

"Well, wife," said Massimo severely, when he finally let go, "What are you preparing for your husband's breakfast?"

"French toast," I replied, going back over to the worktop.

"Oh, great!"

I laughed at Massimo's expression of delight and we looked at each other for a moment; all of a sudden I was conscious of a strange shyness. No, it wasn't a shyness – that presupposed embarrassment and I never felt embarrassed with Massimo. It was more what the Italians called *pudore* – a certain chasteness of feeling, a recognition of the need for delicacy. Wordlessly, we faced each other in our new domestic surroundings, the hint of a smile playing over our faces.

◌

"You've got the cakes, have you?" asked Massimo, locking the car doors and activating the alarm.

"Yes," I replied, showing him the precious load balanced on my extended hand. I squared my shoulders and we walked up his parents' drive together.

Before we got to the front door, it was flung open and Massimo's cousin Laura ran down the steps. "*Ciao, ciao!*"

she cried, flinging her arms around Massimo. "*Ciao Massimino!*" She smiled and then kissed him on both cheeks. "*Ciao* Emma," she added, and brushed my cheeks before running back up the steps in front of us. Her voice was an excited shout disappearing inside the house, "Here they are at last, everybody. The newly-weds!"

The hubbub of voices coming from the dining-room was deafening to my ears. As I paused to hang my coat up in the hall, a horrifying impulse to turn tail and retreat back out the front door swamped me.

"Emma," said Massimo, stroking my face, "are you all right?"

"Yes – yes – of course I am." I managed a short laugh and flicked back my hair from my face.

"You've gone very pale all of a sudden," pressed Massimo, his eyebrows lowered with concern.

"No, I'm fine." I shrugged. "I suppose I must be hungry, that's all."

He took me gently by the arm. "Well, we'll be sitting down to lunch very soon, and –" Whatever he had been about to say was cut short by a booming voice.

"So here you both are!" A man in late middle age was poking his head around the dining-room door. He emerged into the hall with all the celerity that his robust frame would allow for. "The two love birds out hiding in the hall, eh!"

Massimo shot me another questioning glance, and then gave my arm a squeeze. "Uncle Aldo!" he replied, extending his arms for the ritual embrace and kiss on each cheek.

"Welcome home!" cried Uncle Aldo, giving Massimo's shoulder a comradely clap. "Although you're probably sorry to be back from your honeymoon, eh?" He chortled and administered another thump. Then his eyes fastened on mine. "Emma," he greeted me, extending a hand in a show of impeccable formality, "You're looking very well." His eyes slid from my face down to breast level. "As usual, I might add."

"Isn't she?" Massimo smiled happily.

"Shall we go in?" asked Uncle Aldo, indicating the dining-room, "After you both."

As I moved forward to follow in Massimo's wake, dear Uncle Aldo's hand pressed into the small of my back. "Ladies first," he murmured, just behind my ear.

We entered the dining-room and a lull fell on the competing voices. The family was huddled around the table, except for two small girls who were playing with a doll over by the window. I felt my customary unease when faced with a gathering of curious eyes. My fingers tightened on the tray of cakes and I endeavoured to include everyone present in my smile.

"Hello everybody!" said Massimo, and looking around the room, added, "Where's my mother?"

I couldn't see her anywhere either.

Slowly the group of relatives drew apart, revealing the chair on which my mother-in-law was sitting.

"My son!" she breathed, and brought the back of her hand to her mouth, shaking her head. From behind the chair, her daughter Verdiana patted her shoulder.

"*Mamma!*" Massimo went over and bent down to kiss her. My mother-in-law took his face in her hands and looked searchingly at him. She nodded slowly and then let her hands fall listlessly into her lap.

From behind the chair, Verdiana once again patted her shoulder, saying, "Never mind, *mamma,* chin up."

Massimo drew away and looked around him. "How about a bit of jollity for the occasion? The atmosphere here is more funereal than celebratory. What's with you lot?"

A ripple of laughter passed around the room, like the lambent presence of lightning in cobalt blue clouds.

"Just as long as you're happy," said my mother-in-law, her eyes not quite meeting his.

"Yes," echoed Verdiana, "We hope you'll be happy."

"Of course we'll be happy!" Massimo extended an arm, beckoning me to come forward. I went over to the chair to greet my mother-in-law.

"I hope you're feeling well, *signora*," I said, bending to kiss her.

"Ah, it's nothing serious, nothing at all. I had a bit of a turn, but I'm all right."

"Well, that's a relief!" I replied.

"And I suppose you can call me Licia now."

I smiled, confused; it would not be easy to forget how much store my mother-in-law had set by the correct formalities being observed. This included being called *signora* for as long as we'd known each other. Why get carried away with intimacies like first-name terms just because I now had a wedding ring on my finger? Or would that be just another correct and expected observance of the formalities? The tray of cakes started to feel heavy.

"Ah – I was forgetting…"

"Thanks, you shouldn't have."

My father-in-law stepped forward to greet me; there was more shaking of hands and then, turning to the company, he said, "I think it's time we toasted the newly-weds."

A woman's voice broke through the murmurs of assent. "Licia has put herself out for others too much, as usual." My mother-in-law's sister, Mina, was pouring water from a jug into a glass. "She wanted to give you two the best possible welcome home, and now she's feeling the worse for it." Her lips compressed into a thin line as she handed the glass to her sister. "I told you not to go to such trouble Licia, didn't I? What did you want to do it for anyway?" Her eyes glittered darkly like two chips of coal. "You just stay sitting where you are." The eyes flickered in my direction. "It's high time others learnt to muck in and do their fair share."

Out in the garden, I looked around me and blinked in the surprisingly strong sunlight. The sky was a pale blue, with just the slightest veiling of cloud here and there. Late autumn it might be, but the midday temperature was still warm enough to enjoy the aperitifs in a balmy atmosphere that quieted the regret of a dying year. It didn't take long to bring everything out, and soon the family had gathered around the patio table and were helping themselves to the spread of salamis, cheeses and olives.

All of a sudden I was enveloped by a delightful scent, and raised my head in surprise. What was it? My head swivelled here and there and then located what must be the source: a large Japanese medlar coming into full bloom stood in the shade over against the wall. The scent was a heady yet delicate mixture of hawthorn blossom and baby's talcum powder. I walked slowly over to the tree, careful not to spill any of the aperitif from my glass.

But the nearer I moved to it, the more difficult it was to get the scent; right up beside it, I had to bend down a branch and sniff at the white candle of bloom. The effect was cloying. Disappointed, I let the branch go and took a sip from my glass. And a very different smell now insinuated itself in my nostrils: the shadowy earth under the tree and the murky expanse of the evergreen shrubs, untouched by the subdued rays of the sun, gave off an odour of damp decay. Against the wall, climbing roses stretched out brown thorny sprays, rigid in their leaflessness, from which large red hips dangled like muted lanterns in the gloom, the only steadfast witness to their occult splendour, the waiting darkness of the earth.

From under the protective branches of the medlar tree, I paused to observe Massimo's family. There was no doubt about it – they were in their element eating, drinking and talking together.

A child's scream cut through the air, and my eyes flew in the direction of the patio table. The smaller of my sister-in-law's two little girls had tripped and fallen, grazing her knee. She sobbed inconsolably as Verdiana cradled her in her arms, shouting at her husband Pietro to run and get the disinfectant and plasters in the downstairs bathroom. Without a word, Pietro lumbered off into the house on this errand. Meanwhile, the rest of the family gathered round making clucking noises of sympathy. I began to propel myself across the garden – far better to join them speedily rather than continue to lurk like a spectre under the medlar tree – they'd be bound to notice, and it would be taken as Nordic cold-heartedness.

""It's nothing serious, sweetheart," Verdiana was saying, stroking Caterina's tearstained little face. "You'll be up and playing again in no time." Pietro finally reappeared and she turned to him and snapped, "Would you hurry up and give them to me, for God's sake!" Pietro hunkered down and held Caterina's hand while Verdiana disinfected the graze and then applied the plaster.

"Poor little darling," said my mother-in-law.

"She'll be all right, she'll be all right," said my father-in-law, ruffling the little girl's hair.

Caterina's sobs were abating; she had reached the stage where she was giving shuddering little hiccups. I watched

Verdiana soothing her and said, "These falls are inevitable, but it's always upsetting to see a small child in distress."

Verdiana looked up at me. "Yes," she replied, "although a mother always knows how best to cope." She paused to pat Caterina's hair back into place. "You're not a mother, so of course it seems more difficult to you." She stood up and smoothed out the creases in the little girl's dress and let her run back to play with her sister. The men wandered off. "Tell me," Verdiana took up, head aslant, "are you going to keep working now that you're married?"

"Yes," I replied, unhesitatingly. "Of course."

The murmured conversation that had been going on between my mother-in-law and her sister stopped. A look passed among the three of them.

"But," continued Verdiana, her eyes narrowing, "it's not as if my brother doesn't make enough money for both of you to live comfortably on."

Now it was my turn to start flicking my eyes around, in the hopes of catching Massimo's attention. But he was chatting away with his father, Pietro, and Uncle Aldo. "The fact is," I replied, noting the stiltedness in my voice with unease, "that I work because I enjoy working. Interpreting is full of challenges. There's always something new to learn."

"Oh well," my mother-in-law sighed, "some women are just hugely ambitious."

Both older women began to move off arm-in-arm back towards the table. "This new generation of women just takes the biscuit," Aunt Mina's voice floated back.

"And, of course," added my mother-in-law querulously, "these career women are no use at all in the kitchen."

"I know," agreed her sister, "it's all fast food now, isn't it? What is the world coming to!"

Verdiana was looking steadily into the middle distance, but at these words, the faintest of smiles settled on her face.

Silently she moved off, over to where Laura was playing with her two little girls. I glanced at Massimo, but he was laughing at something Pietro had said. Should I move over to where he was and intrude on the men's conversation – Massimo wouldn't mind, but the others would – or should I retreat back to the tree? I couldn't refill my glass – I didn't want to get them going on Nordic drunkenness. What could I do with myself?

An arm wound around my waist and my head swivelled.

"Oh, Massimo –" I smiled in relief.

"Who did you think it would be?" asked Massimo, looking at me quizzically. "Everything all right? Can I get you anything?"

"Um, no – thanks. Everything's just fine." I fiddled with the stem of my glass.

Massimo gave me a hug, and then a quick kiss. "That's great," he said.

"Massimo," called my mother-in-law from the table, "you've missed many things while you were away." She stood up slowly, and drawing Aunt Mina's arm through hers, walked back over towards us.

She paused to regain her breath, placing a hand over her ample bosom, and then announced, "The Vannocchis were burgled ten days ago."

"You're not serious!" exclaimed Massimo.

My mother-in-law cast her eyes to the ground and sighed. A long drawn-out affair that sufficed to focus everyone's attention on her. "Yes," she took up, and sniffed ostentatiously, "The house was cleaned out. I suppose we can only be thankful that no harm was done to anybody – the family were all asleep in bed when it happened."

"I'm sorry to hear that – it must have been a terrible shock for them." said Massimo.

"Of course!" said my mother-in-law, "They had their

life savings hidden in the sitting-room, and that was taken too. Can you imagine!"

"God between us and all harm!" cried Aunt Mina. Her face registered outraged fright. "There are just too many foreigners in Italy – Italy isn't of the Italians any more."

Massimo looked at her. "You mean they know who did it?"

"No," Aunt Mina admitted, "but everyone knows that these interlopers are responsible for the wave of crime sweeping the country."

Massimo laughed softly. "Well, it's been sweeping the country for as long as I can remember – and that includes a time when there were no immigrants."

"No, no, no!" cried my mother-in-law, "these are dreadful times."

Aunt Mina shook her head. "Never seen the like of this."

"But," I blurted out, "you're the generation that's been through the Second World War."

A frozen silence ensued.

My mother-in-law's lips settled into a thin line. "Are you criticizing us?" She clutched Aunt Mina for support.

"Emma didn't want to criticize you, *mamma*," interjected Massimo.

"And after all I've been through," Her voice sank to a whisper.

"You didn't mean anything, sure you didn't?" urged Massimo.

"Of course not," I answered.

My mother-in-law nodded slowly.

"The younger generation," said Aunt Mina quietly, and to no-one in particular, "have no idea how to show respect for their elders."

Then my mother-in-law drew Massimo's arm through hers and patted it. "On the second of November," she said, "for the feast of the Dead, we went to the cemetery."

"We brought enough chrysanthemums for all the family," Aunt Mina added, "and made sure that everyone's grave was clean and tidy."

"We visited them all," said my mother-in-law, a hint of animation creeping into her voice, "Mother, Father, Aunt Franca, Uncle Antonio and Uncle Sandro…"

"And poor young Pasquale," Aunt Mina chipped in, "killed by those terrible Germans…"

"It's a pity you weren't here to come with us," my mother-in-law said, turning to me. "We could have done with a hand."

"Do you keep the feast of the Dead in your country?" enquired Aunt Mina.

"Well," I extemporised, "I think actually that it would be more of a private thing…" My eye fell on Caterina as she ran after her sister, laughing delightedly, her fall now forgotten. Halloween in all its pagan glory flashed through my mind – but how to explain that to them? Pointed witches' hats, masks, night-time bonfires and parties: there didn't seem to be very much common ground with the subdued day-time silence of a cypress-shadowed cemetery and spiky bunches of chrysanthemums. "It's pretty well up to each person when and if they want to visit the graves of their nearest and dearest, I suppose."

There was a moment's silence.

"Who will look after us when we're gone?" my mother-in-law said, pulling her woollen cardigan closer around her. "Who's going to continue doing what we've always done for ours?"

I looked at my mother-in-law for a moment, unable to think of a suitable answer. A situation that was afflicting me increasingly. Then there was a shout from the group of men. "Well everybody," cried Uncle Aldo, making pointed gestures at his watch, "time for lunch, wouldn't you think?" He was backed up by my father-in-law and Pietro.

"Oh lord!" My mother-in-law looked at her watch. "It's got so late!

"I'll give you a hand," said Aunt Mina. They both headed off purposefully. Massimo began to follow in their wake and, turning back to smile, beckoned to me with his head.

I watched as the family trooped bit by bit into the dining-room; silence descended over the emptied garden. The rumble of chatter coming from inside the house reached my ears as if from a great distance. On a nearby shrub, a spider's web oscillated like a miniature trampoline in a sudden breath of wind; with delicate grace, the spider poised at its centre flexed long probing legs, now on the alert. The dining-room window was flung open, bringing a wave of noise with it; an affronted squawk from a blackbird that zig-zagged in alarm across the garden was a liquid dagger through the shroud of silence.

Massimo stuck his head out. "Emma, are you coming in?"

IN HINDSIGHT

"What kept you until now?" His wife closes the front door on the wind and rain outside. Her irritation is palpable. She takes his briefcase and then removes his coat. "How did you get so wet?" she grumbles, shaking the coat, "you'd think you'd been out wandering the roads." She pauses, and then casts him a sidelong glance before hanging the coat to dry near the radiator in the hall.

He ignores all but the first question. "You know how things build up before Christmas," he says quietly, "and I've explained to you how busy I am with the exhibition." He picks up his briefcase and begins to head towards the study.

"This kind of thing – it's not like you."

The unmistakable note of accusation stops him in his tracks. He steels himself and turns slowly back to her.

"You haven't forgotten that the Niccolais are coming round this evening," she probes, observing him intently.

He feels himself go limp. Of course he'd bloody forgotten. How is he going to face them?

"No," he replies in the same level tone as before, "I hadn't forgotten." His eyes attempt to hold hers, but they withstand the penetrating gaze for only a moment before sliding down to the level of her shoulder. "How long have

I got before they arrive?" he asks, forcing his eyes back into the beam of his wife's watchful stare.

"Three-quarters of an hour," she informs him crisply.

"Well – " he falters. What the hell is he going to say? "Well," he reiterates, injecting a dose of firmness into his voice, "there are a few loose ends still need to be tied up for the exhibition on Monday. Give me half an hour, then I'll go and freshen up. That all right?"

There is an edgy diffidence in the slant of his wife's head as she regards him. She nods slowly.

He closes the study door behind him and sags against it in the dark. He can feel her eyes boring into him through the door. His hand scrabbles for the light switch and turns it on.

He needs a drink. He needs several drinks. He needs to down at least five whiskies in rapid succession until that peculiar tightness in his chest loosens its grip on him. But he'll have to wait. It wouldn't do for the host to lurch out to greet his guests already rat-arsed.

He moves towards the desk. Distractedly he begins to empty the contents of his briefcase onto it. Not a heart attack, for God's sake. At forty-one. No – damn it to hell – he knows it isn't a heart attack. His eyes fall on the paraphernalia from work spread out in front of him. The phone bill from the gallery; a report on the Bartoli exhibition, which has to be gone through; a handwritten memo. The pain in his chest gives a sudden kick.

That handwriting. Unusual, elegant. Like her. He groans quietly.

There in front of him is the letter opener. His hand closes around the ivory handle, and he spears the handwritten memo savagely with its sharp point. He holds it up for inspection, twirling the handle round, and then with his other hand snatches it off and crushes it into a ball. Pain comes from the hand holding the letter opener: his fingers have clamped onto the blade. Blood seeps through.

Two of his fingers have been sliced. He looks at them in disgust. Then he looks at the crushed memo. He smoothes it out on the desk, trying not to smear it with blood.

He gets unsteadily to his feet, still clutching the memo, and heads for the armchair. He has twenty-five minutes to get a grip before facing his wife and their guests.

Slowly he brings the memo up to eye level. The tone is impressively detached and professional. Meeting tomorrow Friday at 19.00 for Bartoli's *vernissage*… Discuss the layout and order of the paintings… Arrangements for a wine reception…

Then he comes to the signature. Sibilla. His head falls back slowly on the armchair and he stares up at the clock. The note slips from his lax fingers. Sibilla. Sibilla Malaspina. Who is the person she has suddenly metamorphosed into? What has happened to the person she seemed to be just a day and a night ago?

What has happened to him…

An image surfaces of himself in his office yesterday morning after he'd picked up the post on the way in. He'd spotted her note immediately, but put off reading it. Kidding himself again that it could wait its turn, that there was no need to give it any preferential treatment. He'd got round to reading it all right, but even then he'd been blasé. Full of a risible sense of omnipotence. Of his unquestionable ability to maintain control over his life.

In hindsight, they were the last moments of his previous existence. The last moments of an organised, secure, well worked-out existence. He will never have moments like them again: how can he extricate himself from this mess in any shape that might resemble his old self?

When she first came to work at the gallery, did he have any inkling of how events would turn out? He closes his eyes the better to concentrate, and thinks back to September. She was recommended to him by a colleague who had been very impressed with her professionalism. In bed or the office? Jesus! He bends forward and covers his face with his hands. Then he rubs the palm of his uncut hand back and forth over his forehead in an effort to ease the tension.

That way lies madness. He can't start wondering whether she's seduced every man she's ever come in contact with.

He sits back in the armchair and once again casts his mind back to September. It had been obvious that he was going to need a hand with Bartoli's exhibition in December. After the early years of his professional life in the monetary wilderness, his gallery had been increasing steadily in prestige; he knew this exhibition was the means that would let him make the leap forward into the big-time league. The memory of his initial struggles to make ends meet was like a whip that occasionally flicked into vicious life, sending shock waves of pain and worry scurrying over his skin.

Armed only with his honours degree in art history, he and his girlfriend – now his wife – had come to Florence, where he was to pursue a post-graduate qualification on Fra Angelico. They both fell in love with the place. His wife had put her degree in English to use and got herself a job slogging in one of the private language schools in the city. But things had been very tight. He had cycled all over the city, and out of it, in all weather, giving private lessons in people's homes. The austere Renaissance *palazzi* right in the centre of the city with their frescoed ceilings; bland apartments in the residential areas; those well-to-do art nouveau villas mounting Viale Macchiavelli in turreted state, with the cypress trees winding round the graceful curves in the

10$ pages

287 pp

= 28,987 words

Pillar Press

30 pages Plus synopsis

Pillar Press
Ladywell

Thomastown, Co Kilkenny

road like dark ticker tape. He had wanted to paint, but some reticence in him blocked the flow. He became aware of a certain foolishness in the enterprise. Gradually the practicalities of existence took over.

Then came the idea of the gallery. How well he remembered the apartment belonging to the poet he had been teaching; the poet who loved painting. The walls of which were so crowded with paintings, that new acquisitions were kept stacked on the floor, piling up in every room. That gave him the idea: a place where paintings could be viewed properly. A Gallery. But not in Florence, which was already saturated. In Pisa. His eye was good, he and his wife both knew how to make and keep contacts – bit by bit they'd make their way.

So he wasn't in the business of leaving anything to chance. That was why he had taken on Sibilla – in order to have someone who knew how to liaise with painters and network with the media, while he got on with the finances and logistics of the whole thing.

Yes – the first time he had ever set eyes on her was still a vivid memory. A tell-tale detail that, which should have alerted him to impending trouble. Although, in fairness, maybe the very doggedness with which he'd refused to attribute any importance to the impression she had made on him was an even more telling detail.

He'd called her for an informal interview one afternoon in late September and she had arrived punctually. He'd been sitting at his desk in the office when she knocked on the door, opening it a fraction.

"Hello," she said, sticking her head around it, "my name's Sibilla Malaspina. I believe you're expecting me." Then she smiled. The atmosphere in the office seemed to liquefy, beginning to shift and roll in lapping wavelets. All of a sudden, he felt defensive.

"Yes, that's right," he replied coolly, "Come in and take a seat." He gave her only the most cursory of glances as she walked across the room, but what he saw in that one glance was indeed striking. She was tall, slender, of an indefinable age, although she must have been in her thirties. Shoulder-length straight black hair framing a pale ivory complexion. And a face of unusual beauty.

His hackles went up. For God's sake – the last thing he needed on his payroll was an airhead. He whipped out her CV. "Now," he said brusquely, "let's have a look at this, shall we?"

He had been taken aback at the CV. *Summa cum laude* in art history from Pisa, a Master's at the Sorbonne, and a list of work experience that was impressive. Just what he required in fact. He began to question her, and as she answered – very succinctly he noted, and in excellent English, which would be great for international contacts – his irritation partly subsided. What was she but another career woman, and as such he was perfectly prepared to give her the respect that was her due.

The details of her qualifications and experience having been got through, he then asked her how she would cope with the inevitable delays that Bartoli was bound to cause, given his character. How would she envisage keeping him to his deadlines? He sat back, crossed one leg over his knee, and folded his arms. As she replied, he finally allowed himself to observe her steadily.

She wasn't his type. True, she was good-looking enough. But he'd always liked his women in the Botticelli mould, and she was very far from anything like that. There was something slightly disturbing about her colouring, something polarized, unresolved, in such a marked contrast between her black hair and the paleness of her skin. Yes – now he had it. That painting by Klimt. She reminded him of *The Dancer*. He looked away.

He'd given her the job of course. And as time passed, he found that she was a discreet presence who got things done quietly and efficiently. He liked this discretion. But he was also surprised by it. In taking her on he'd had a vague expectation of trouble in the offing – which had made him determined to keep her at a civil distance. And the civiler the better. He'd thought there would be a little more ego making itself felt, maybe; a little more of the *prima donna* syndrome. But he'd had to admit that it wasn't there. So he let his guard down slightly with her, stopping to talk now and again, and found that he could make her laugh. She had a lovely smile.

Things were going along swimmingly with Bartoli as well, who was responding positively to Sibilla and keeping to his deadlines with reasonable punctuality. All things considered though, he was glad not to have too much direct contact with Bartoli any more. Whenever he'd met up with him previously, he'd always come away feeling unsettled. Take the place where Bartoli lived – it was more like a bloody encampment than anything else. Bartoli rarely met people anywhere but at home, and the reason for this particular quirk continued to elude him. If he were Bartoli, he would be glad to get out of it as often as possible.

Bartoli lived in a rundown *casale* up in the Lunigiana, just outside one of those villages perched so precariously on the ridge of a mountain. It was at the same time beautiful, isolated and disquieting. The inhabitants of the area were a strange lot; they too seemed to be struggling with some inner balancing act. What kind of people could dream up such pretty houses, only to make them cling so grimly to mountains – mountains whose heaving outlines made them look as if they were trying to shrug off those little blobs of pink and white and orange that spilled and dribbled down their sheer dark sides, tenaciously fighting the force of gravity every inch of the way. This was seismic territory. But there you had it – the artist was attached to his habitat and the laity had to make their way there if they wished to meet him.

There was also the alarming chaos that fell on him like a paralysing weight every time he had stepped over the threshold of Bartoli's *casale*. The mildewed walls, the cobwebbed windows, the lack of furniture; the trail of paw marks left by the huge dog he kept, sheets of old newspaper strewn everywhere, and books littered to right left and centre. The huge *damigiane* of rocket-fuel that passed itself off as red wine, unopened ones thrown together with the empties; plates with the remains of days-old snacks adorning various surfaces, as did clothes, ashtrays, cups, glasses and mugs.

This bedlam was the talk of the scandalized village, and anyone who had anything to do with Bartoli was automatically tarred with the same disreputable bohemian brush.

But Bartoli was indeed a fine artist, headed for success. He hoped to assist him there, and in doing so, find his own secure niche in the world of art. They were both in or about the same age, moving in the same world, but on parallel lines. Sometimes when he looked at Bartoli's paintings, he wondered what it took to create such originality. What was it in the man enabled him to crystallise energy on a canvas? He respected him for this. Was prepared to admire him too. Although, he had to admit that a part of him envied Bartoli this mark of divine preferment: it was the part of him he knew would never take the risks that Bartoli took. Bartoli and those like him were lightning conductors – very beneficial for a mostly grateful mankind, but at an enormous price. The exposed, disordered, fundamentally debilitating life that Bartoli led was not on the agenda for him. He could understand it in theory, even go along with it up to a certain point; but there was something histrionic about the way chaos was so actively sought out and embraced that repelled him. It was unnecessary. So while he'd never reach Bartoli's heights, neither would he have to sink to his depths. He was carving out his own safe, secure niche, and in the process saving himself a lot of bother and trouble.

Monday mornings, at a certain point, began to weigh less on him. He'd get in at a quarter to nine and wait for the wave of vitality that Sibilla brought with her when she breezed in on the dot of nine. There were times when it was nice just to look at her – as long, of course, as she didn't realise she was being observed. At unexpected moments her face would acquire a wistful quality that set him wondering.

He also found himself pondering her relationship with Bartoli. She had certainly made a go of her role as mediator between Bartoli and the outside world, and it was evident that he must trust and esteem her. This was in marked contrast to *his* more fraught relations with the man. What kind of a person was she really? There must be more to her than the efficient exterior she presented to the world, because if that were all it took to win Bartoli's confidence, then he should have been in pole position long ago. Instead, he knew that Bartoli had played around with him, skipping appointments, not coming up with the goods… This hadn't happened with Sibilla. Of course, there was always the fact that they came from the same country, and the same part of the country at that, although from opposite ends of the social scale: Sibilla's medieval warlord ancestors had held sway over all that harsh terrain from their impregnable mountain stronghold in the town of Massa.

Bartoli's first major consignment of paintings was due three weeks before the exhibition, with the second coming ten days later. That would then leave Sibilla and himself time to work out the order and the layout. This consignment was a test case of how smoothly the rest of the operation would go, and he'd been pretty uptight about it. But in the event, everything went off without a hitch.

He had been in his office when he heard her arriving back at the gallery the evening of the consignment. He came to the door and listened to her as she directed the van driver and his assistant in Italian on where to deposit Bartoli's carefully wrapped paintings. She was looking exceptionally well and radiated a happy vibrancy. He turned around and headed back to his desk.

When all the paintings had been unloaded, she came to the door and, with a smile on her face, said, "Well – are you not curious to see what Bartoli has in store for us?"

"Let's have a look then," he replied, getting up from the desk and following her out to the gallery.

Between them, they removed the wrappings from the paintings, lining them up against the walls. Then they stood back near the entrance and observed them in silence. He was the first to speak.

"Yes, I think we're home and dry," he said, nodding.

"Good," she answered, glancing at him. "I certainly like what I see – there's no doubting the quality."

"Quite."

Another silence followed, and then she took up, "They seem to fall into two categories. Would you agree?"

"Yes. And it's more than just chronology: I think Bartoli is being pulled in two directions."

"Aren't we all," murmured Sibilla.

He shot a glance at her, but she was gazing intently at the paintings.

"Which type do you prefer?" he asked, suddenly curious to see what her reaction to them would be. She considered for a moment, and then said, "I prefer the more abstract ones. For their colours mainly, but for the brush strokes too, they're more confident. Even though he's taken greater risks."

He had known that she was going to choose those paintings, but was still disturbed to hear it enunciated so – well, so definitively.

"Which ones do you prefer?" she then asked, turning her eyes on him. He was momentarily fazed by the peculiar glitter that lit them from within. "I prefer the other ones," he said curtly, turning away. He folded his arms and surveyed the paintings. "I like their plain-speaking colours and the honest energy they possess."

She didn't reply. He glanced at her. The corners of her mouth had turned up in an irritatingly enigmatic little smile, and she was taking out a notebook. Then she moved off and started to take down the name of each painting. He felt strangely put out. Well, maybe he'd been too abrupt.

"Listen," he said, moving over beside her, "it's been a pretty demanding day. Do you want to come for an aperitif before heading off home?"

Again, she hadn't replied immediately. There followed a long still moment.

"And why not?" she said eventually, putting away her notebook, "Where shall we go?" She hadn't looked at him.

The wine bar in Piazza delle Vettovaglie was full of people, the weather being too cold for sitting outside. The counter was laden with *stuzzichini*, little mouthfuls that complemented the selection of wines on offer. He went for a glass of full-bodied Tuscan red, and she opted for a glass of the *novello*. He filled a plate of *stuzzichini* for both of them and they sat down at a table in the adjoining room. Conversation wasn't easy because of the loud music, but by the time he had refilled his glass twice, things had got onto an easier footing. This despite the fact that Sibilla was still nursing the same glass of *novello*. Like a lot of Italian women, she didn't drink much. They got around to talking about their initial impressions of each other.

"You projected an aura of assurance," said Sibilla, "you were pretty sure of your ideas."

"Uh-huh," He wondered if she was going to tell him what the substance behind the aura was.

But she just glanced at him before taking another sip of her wine. "So how did I fare with you?"

He didn't feel like being honest with her though. "I thought you seemed very efficient," he replied stiltedly. "I was – pleased – about that…"

"Oh, right," she said, and her eyes held his a fraction longer than they should have. "It's all part of your passion for – what was it – honest energy…"

He allowed himself a smile.

∽

There had been no repetition of their evening in the wine bar. But over the next few days, as he worked steadily towards the approaching deadline, her eyes, as they had held his in the wine bar, would suddenly and unsettlingly impinge on his paperwork. That playfully challenging look they had had about them. Teasing, almost. He tried to banish them from his mind, but something in him was provoked by them. He'd had a glimpse of yet another side to her that just wouldn't go away. And it had become difficult not to be sidetracked by this when they were working together. There was a noticeable tension in the air between them now that he was acutely aware of, but powerless to dispel. This in its turn intensely irritated him, and he found himself avoiding her.

The day of Bartoli's second consignment arrived, and passed off without incident. He was greatly relieved by this, but once again Sibilla seemed to have pulled off a miracle.

Then he had received her note asking for a meeting late on the Friday before the exhibition. Details had to be finalised. They got down to work, and it was quite late when Sibilla finally stood up from the desk and ran a hand through her hair.

"Well, I'm glad that's sorted," she said.

The tension had relaxed between them, so he suggested a late dinner. They'd both put in a lot of hard work, and, well, they deserved it, didn't they?

They chose a restaurant near the theatre. It was convenient, and served until late.

By the time they had ordered their *antipasti* and had a glass of the excellent *prosecco*, he knew he was in deep trouble. There was something compelling, something mesmeric about Sibilla that evening and he couldn't take his eyes off her. He was aware also that his eyes, as they lingered on her mouth, were anything but chaste. But he didn't care. A certain dreaminess had come into her eyes and her movements had acquired a languor that aroused him. He was waylaid by a jumble of sensations that he couldn't begin to put into coherent thought. So he didn't even try. All he knew was that she was beautiful. And he desired her.

At a certain point Sibilla stood up. "I'm going to the ladies," she said, and disappeared out towards the back. Then, suddenly, he got to his feet too. He had no clear idea of what he was going to do, but he didn't want to continue sitting here with her. Some kind of action was called for. He quickly paid their bill and waited for her at the door. Shortly afterwards he saw Sibilla making her way towards him. She looked at him questioningly.

"I thought we might move on somewhere else," he said. "If that's all right by you."

How he could still see that face turning towards him, as if in slow motion, the lips of that full mouth parted slightly, and those eyes. It was as if he was seeing them truly for the first time. Grey green eyes that looked right at him. Right into him.

But she said nothing.

He took her by the elbow and steered her out the door.

They both cried out as a blast of cold air hit them. Sibilla tried hurriedly to close her coat. "Right," he said, "what places would still be open? Where could we go for a night cap?"

"Let me think."

She began to saunter up the narrow winding street, and he followed, their heels clicking against the large cobble-stones in a slack counterpoint that echoed in the frozen silence. Suddenly Sibilla turned to him. "I've really enjoyed this evening." she said.

The light from a silver moon came falling slowly through the frosty air onto her upturned face, and a spurt of happiness shot through him. He felt alive. Ready to take on the world.

His arm encircled her waist and pulled her to him. He cupped her head and drew her face near to his. He ran his cheek over the cool pale satin of her cheek, breathing in her scent. And then he kissed her.

After a while she pulled away and regarded him.

"Sibilla," he said, "you're the most beautiful thing has happened to me in a long time. Don't leave me on my own tonight."

Her head was lowered, so he couldn't see her expression. And still she said nothing. 'Don't say no,' he thought frantically, 'Please don't say no.'

Suddenly she looked up and smiled at him. "Come back to my place," she said simply.

He awoke with a start, and couldn't get his bearings. The room was in complete darkness. In a rush of anxiety he turned his head slightly to the left, to where it seemed that a window framed a rectangle of less intense blackness. But there shouldn't have been a window to his left. Then the memory slid back over him like a wave from a tropical sea. Sibilla. He reached out a hand and encountered her sleeping form. Smooth, creamy skin. A sense of wonder took hold of him, and he smiled to himself in the dark hushed stillness of her bedroom.

Unexpectedly, insidiously, a sense of unease seeped into this pleasure. What time was it? Cautiously, he eased himself into a sitting position and looked around for a clock. He couldn't make one out anywhere. He got out of the bed, careful not to disturb Sibilla, and winced at the coldness of the tiled floor under his bare feet. His mobile was in his trouser pocket. That would tell him the time. He drew back the curtain on the window and, slanting the phone to catch what little light made its way in through the slats of the shutters, switched it on. Three-seventeen. Damn it. Damn it anyway. And there were two missed calls from his wife. What was he going to do now? What would he say to her? She would have been worried. Troubled, he let the curtain fall back into place.

There was a muffled sound from the bed, and then Sibilla turned over and reached out to the light on the bedside table. There was a click and a subdued pinkish hue brought the room into dim focus. She propped herself up on one elbow and rubbed her eyes, blinking.

"What's up?" she asked.

He felt a sudden rush of shame, for his nakedness, for his thoughts, and for the bloody awful mess he'd created. He walked back over to the bed and slid into it again, pulling the covers up around him.

"It's very late," he said, and then glanced at her.

She pulled the covers up around herself as well and turned to look at him. "Already having regrets, are we?"

"No, no" he replied quickly, "it's not that." He rubbed his chin and a rasping noise echoed around the unfamiliar bedroom. But it *was* that, of course. What a mess.

"Switch off the light, Sibilla." he said. The words resounded unpleasantly and were then swallowed by the silence, like stones thudding into a dark bottomless pool.

◊

Outside it still hadn't got bright. The frosted orange glow of the street lamps hung limply in the cold air, rebuffed by the uniform cloud coverage of a murky sky. He paced up and down the small kitchen, clutching his mobile. What should he do? Should he ring her or not? He looked at it dubiously for the umpteenth time and shook his head. He turned around to pace back to the other side, and saw Sibilla standing at the kitchen door. She was belting her dressing gown.

Without saying a word, she glanced at the mobile. Then she started filling the mocha coffee pot; she remained with her back to him, staring out at the lowering sky.

The tension had returned between them, but it wasn't the vibrant tension that comes in the face of the unknown; it was the tension that follows in the wake of the known. Sullen, unyielding. He looked down at his shoes.

The gurgle from the coffee pot tore through the silence. Sibilla turned to look at it, but she didn't move. He regarded her for a moment, her face half averted, its expression serious and drawn. And a pain jagged through him. There were so many things that he wanted to say to her, so many things that needed to be said. Instead he remained silent.

Suddenly she turned to him. "We'd better get this cleared up, hadn't we?" she said briskly. She turned off the gas under the coffee pot. All he could do was look at her. "It's obvious that the whole thing has been a bad idea," she continued in the same hard tone.

"No, no," he cut in, "it's not that it was a bad idea." He paused and made an imploring gesture with his hands. "It's that – I should have called my wife…" His voice trailed away.

She nodded with slow deliberation. "So you're feeling guilty about your wife now. Well," she continued, her voice rising, "you should have thought about that *before* you slept with me. Not *after.*"

They stood facing each other in front of the kitchen window looking out onto a darkened world, like two actors frozen under a spotlight on stage. He looked away, rubbing the stubble on his chin. She continued to look at him, and he was acutely aware of her mounting anger. He buckled under the weight of what had to be said, and remained mute.

"I think it's time you went home to your wife," said Sibilla. She paused for a moment and enunciated carefully, "You just won't do." Then sharply, "So that's that." The expression of scorn that settled on her face seared through him.

"Sibilla," he pleaded, "let's not say anything we might regret later. Why don't we – "

"Look," she cut in, "there won't be a later. Actions speak louder than words."

"This will all seem very different on Monday morning. Give me time…"

She paused to look at him. "You know," she took up, a glint coming into her eyes, "it might be no harm if I handed in my notice."

He looked at her, appalled.

"After all," she continued, "everything's organised for the exhibition. You don't actually need me any more." She turned towards the kitchen door and added quietly, "And I certainly don't need you."

~

The door to her apartment had closed on him and, as if in a trance, he had somehow got the lift downstairs and gone out onto the street. He couldn't for the life of him remember where he had parked his car yesterday. The car was somewhere else, it belonged to another era, and he couldn't find his way back to it.

He wandered aimlessly for what seemed like hours, and eventually turned into via S. Francesco. An icy wind whipped at his coat and low slate-grey clouds scudded across the sky. The severely pruned trees lining the road poked bare black branches like gnarled walking sticks into the sky, as if in a futile attempt to catch the tattered trails of the clouds.

His fingers came in contact with the mobile in his coat pocket, and closed over it. He took it out, and then looked at his watch. No, it wasn't that late. What would he say to his wife? He closed his eyes for a moment and grimaced. Better ring her before he lost his nerve. He'd think of something as he went along.

"What happened you?" she asked, her tone one of worry mixed with annoyance and relief.

"Listen, Bartoli consigned the last of his paintings yesterday evening, and I had to go and collect them. We had a session at his house to celebrate. It got way out of hand. I was in no state to drive."

"Oh," A pause. "But surely you could have rung and let me know."

"Yeah, I'm sorry. But I got really rotten and just didn't think."

She sighed. "Okay. But don't forget – "

"I've got to go now – I'm really busy. See you later."

He turned the mobile off and stuffed it back into his coat pocket. As he walked over towards Piazza S. Caterina, it started to rain; gusting sheets of icy rain that stung his face. The dead leaves hanging onto the immense plane trees encircling the piazza rattled and clicked in the wind, and the fruit balls dangled on their stalks like a travesty of a decorated Christmas tree. He stood there in the rain for an age, oblivious to the cold and wet, paralysed by an immense ache that tormented him, as if he'd suffered some terrible internal injury unbeknownst to himself, and it was flooding his being with pain. Then it stopped raining and he moved off, driven by a fear that he might turn to stone. He tramped up and down the narrow streets with their tall shuttered buildings, looking at the pale watery reflection of the sky in the puddles and the slippery black surface of the roads. Then out onto the *Lungarno*. He stood on *Ponte della Fortezza* and watched as innumerable darts of sleet pocked the sludgy surface of the river. A seagull wheeled above him; its keening was blown away in the darkening air.

What had he done, what had he done?

As the gloaming lengthened and deepened over the town, he braced himself for the journey home. He pulled up at the end of his road and parked the car there. Darkness was now complete and in the cocooned quietness of the car, he sat observing his house from a distance. He saw his wife come into the *salotto* and switch on a hand lamp. She retreated from view, but her shadow jumped briefly over the wall, and then disappeared.

What had she done to him? He no longer knew who he was. He didn't understand. He didn't understand at all.

There is a rap on the study door.

"Richard," comes his wife's voice from outside, "Richard, it's time for you to go and get changed."

"Right, okay."

He continues to stare blankly at the door as the orderly ticking of the clock echoes hollowly in his ears.

FRIENDS OF PILLAR PRESS

Sue Bowden. Andy Bowden. All That Glisters, Thomastown. Margaret Carey. Shem Caulfield. Maura Dieren. Gina O'Donnell. Eva Lynch. Murphy's Bar, Thomastown. Eoin McEvitt. Conor MacGabhann. Helen MacGabhann. Sean O'Neill. Brid O'Neill. Damien Wedge. Colm O'Boyle. Eileen O'Neill. Sean Mahon. Antoinette O'Neill. Aine O'Neill. Frank Neenan. James Hanley. Orla Dukes. Maeve O'Neill. Shane O'Toole. Debra Bowden. Tony Spooner. Elizabeth Cunningham. Richard McLoughlin. Kathryn Potterton. Cormac Buggy. Fiona Shannon.

To become a friend of Pillar Press please contact us at

Ladywell
Thomastown
Co. Kilkenny

Tel: 056-7724901   E-mail: info@pillarpress.ie